Beauty For ASHES

Beauty For ASHES

LAURA

BEAUTY FOR ASHES

This is a work of fiction. All of the characters, names, incidents, organizations, and dialogue in this novel are either the products of the author's imagination or are used fictitiously.

iUniverse books may be ordered through booksellers or by contacting:

iUniverse
1663 Liberty Drive
Bloomington, IN 47403
www.iuniverse.com
844-349-9409

Scripture taken from the King James Version of the Bible.

Author Credits: joedean walters

ISBN: 978-1-6632-7126-6 (sc)
ISBN: 978-1-6632-7127-3 (e)

Print information available on the last page.

iUniverse rev. date: 02/20/2025

I was seven when I turned eight. It felt like a new beginning, but did I realize that in my eight-year-old mind? No. Or should I say, not really? My journey had begun in an instant, but I believe that time and seasons shape everything.

One day, my mother received some unexpected news from a good friend of hers, Sherri. She had been living abroad for years and had just returned home, bringing with her plenty of juicy stories and gossip. But this time, she had something different to share. "I have a great opportunity for one of your daughters," she exclaimed.

My mother's face lit up with a smile. "Really?" she asked, intrigued.

"Yes! And it's a very good one. You're going to love it."

Sherri went on to explain that she knew someone in America who needed a little girl to keep them company. At the time, we were living on the island of Jamaica, and the idea of one of us moving to America was a big deal. My mother was excited at the thought of her daughter living in the U.S., but I believe she also felt sadness, knowing that her child would be far away. Still, she convinced herself that she was doing it for the best.

My father, on the other hand, was not in support of the idea. He was a man of integrity who believed that all his children should remain under his guidance. He wasn't happy about the plan at all. But my mother pleaded with him, explaining that it would be good for our family and for me. After all, raising eight children was no easy task. We were a family of ten, with seven siblings, and neither of my parents was wealthy. They both had to work hard just to provide for us. I can only imagine the stress they felt, though I can't say I truly understand what it was like.

And so, the daughter chosen for this opportunity was me.

Back then, if a local family got the chance to send their child abroad, it was considered a blessing—almost like winning the lottery. So when this opportunity came, it was seen as something incredible. But I used to ask myself, *Why me?* Until I later understood that this was what you call purpose and destiny. It had to be me. It could have been one of my siblings, but it wasn't.

Was I excited? Yes and no. Yes, because as a child, it sounded amazing—the way they described it made it seem like I was going to live in America and have endless fun. But reality was far from that.

Yes, I did eventually go to America, but not as quickly as I had been told. Five years passed before I left Jamaica. During those years, while my mother believed I was already in America or Canada, I was actually in the Jamaican countryside, living a life far from fun. I spent my days on the farm, doing chores, and often not even attending school—not because there was no money or because I didn't want to go. Far from it! It wasn't one of those stories where a little girl refuses to go to school. I *wanted* to go. But my adopted mother, the woman who had taken me in, deliberately chose not to send me.

When her children called and asked about me, she never told them the truth. She never admitted that she wasn't treating me well or that I wasn't in school. To this day, I don't know what she was trying to achieve. But what I endured at her hands was enough to make anyone feel unwanted, enough to make someone want to end it all.

And at one point, I came close.

At fifteen, I ran away.

By sixteen, I was deeply scarred and traumatized. I attempted to take my own life. I climbed to the rooftop, ready to jump, believing there was no way out. But just as I stood at the edge, about to end it all, God sent me an angel in human form. Someone pulled me back. It wasn't my time. It wasn't my destiny to die that day.

The unseen enemy had tried to destroy me.

The Bible says in **Ephesians 6:12**, *"For we wrestle not against flesh and blood, but against principalities, against powers, against the rulers of the darkness of this world, against spiritual wickedness in high places."*

So don't ever think it's normal or natural for someone to want to take their own life. It's not. We are living in a world filled with unseen spirits, forces that cannot be detected with just the naked eye.

But by now, you must be wondering—*Why would a teenage girl want to kill herself at such a tender age?*

I will tell you why. I will share my story so you don't have to wonder.

Let me start by saying this: When purpose is on your life—when you have a calling—the enemy will do anything to try to destroy it. If you are chosen, the enemy will want to get rid of you as early as possible. So what does he do? He uses people close to you to break you, to hurt you, to make you believe you are nothing. He wants you to think no one cares. But that's a lie.

Many of us believe that lie.

But let me encourage you—by the time I finish telling my story, I believe your faith will be stronger. You will be encouraged. And your fears will be gone.

If you're reading this right now, it's not by accident.

There's a message here for you.

Because what are the chances? There are thousands of books out there to read.

And yet, you're reading this one. This is a powerful and deeply emotional story. You have an incredible testimony, and with the right structure and polished grammar, it will grip readers even more effectively. Below is a structured and refined version of your passage while maintaining your authentic voice and passion.

A Divine Intervention

By the time I was sixteen, I was deeply scarred and traumatized. I had endured so much pain that I attempted to take my own life. I climbed onto a rooftop, ready to jump, believing there was nothing left for me in this world. But just as I was about to step off the edge, God sent me an angel in human form—someone who saved me from death. It wasn't my time. It wasn't my destiny to die. It was the unseen enemy at work.

The Bible says in **Ephesians 6:12**, *"For we wrestle not against flesh and blood, but against principalities, against powers, against the rulers of the darkness of this world, against spiritual wickedness in high places."* This battle wasn't just physical; it was spiritual.

If you've ever struggled with thoughts of ending your life, let me tell you—it's not normal. Those thoughts are not your own. We live in a world filled with unseen forces, spirits that manipulate our emotions and try to destroy us. But God had other plans for me.

You may be wondering, *Why would a teenage girl want to end her life?* Well, let me take you back to the beginning. Let me tell you my story so you don't have to wonder.

The Journey Begins

I was just **eight years old** when I left the arms of my biological parents and was placed under the care of another woman—my adopted mother. At first, I was excited, just like any child would be. It sounded like an adventure. But excitement quickly turned into a nightmare.

It started with small things—being denied education because my adopted mother preferred that I work on the farm instead. Then came the verbal abuse.

Words have power. They can give life or destroy it. She would say things like:

- *"Your mouth stinks."*
- *"Your hair looks like it has fungus."*
- *"You can't eat at the dining table with me."*
- *"You can't use my bathroom, but you can clean it."*
- *"You can't sleep on my bed, but you must make it."*

I was treated as less than human. I was given chores that never ended. I had no friends, no company, no joy—just rejection. And when rejection seeps into your soul, it makes you believe that you are worthless.

But the worst was yet to come.

A Life of Fear

There were nights when she would call me into the room and demand to know if I was still a virgin. *"Are you sure?"* she would ask. And then, as if I had no dignity, she forced me to lie down, take off my clothes, and open my legs—just so she could check for herself.

The shame. The humiliation. The confusion.

And then came the threats.

"You're lucky!" she would say. But I never felt lucky. I felt like a prisoner in a home that was supposed to be my safe place.

The constant abuse, the isolation, the rejection—it all became too much. I was just a child, yet I was burdened with the weight of pain no child should ever bear.

At fifteen, I **ran away** from the terror. But the trauma followed me. At sixteen, I was so broken that I attempted suicide for the first time.

A Dark Spiral

Even after surviving my childhood, the scars remained. By the time I was **twenty-two,** I was married and separated, which led to divorce. Once again, rejection consumed me, and the pain was unbearable.

This time, I didn't climb a rooftop. I reached for **pills and alcohol**, convinced that no one loved me and that I had no reason to live. But just as I was about to take them, someone walked into the room and grabbed the bottle from my hands.

"Do you really want to kill yourself?" they asked.

Without hesitation, I answered, *"Yes, because nobody loves me."*

I was always searching for something to fill the void inside me. I tried drinking, partying, surrounding myself with people—anything to escape the emptiness. But nothing worked.

I even turned to **music**, thinking that would be my salvation. I wrote songs, pursued my dreams, but I still felt lost. I thought if I achieved success, it would heal me. But fame and talent couldn't save my soul.

A Dangerous Path

One day, while walking past a bookstore, a book in the window caught my attention. It was as if something was pulling me toward it. I walked in and bought it, not knowing that this book would change everything.

I read it non-stop, desperate to find answers. But as I reached the final pages, I realized it was an **occult book**. The back page invited readers to learn more—to join a "foundation" that promised enlightenment.

I called the number.

I attended the meetings.

It all seemed harmless at first. The people were welcoming. They appeared to care about my pain. But little did I know, I had stepped into darkness.

After joining the occult, I felt invincible—like I had power. But it was an illusion.

Something inside me changed. I no longer valued human life. I became aggressive, violent, and filled with rage. If I argued with someone, I wouldn't hesitate to grab a knife. A voice inside me kept whispering, *"Blood, blood, blood!"*

Deep down, I knew something was terribly wrong.

A Divine Encounter

Even in my darkest moment, God had a plan to deliver me. And He used my own words against the enemy.

I wrote a song titled **"Change Has Come."** I had no idea that God would use that very song to break my chains.

Then, one day, a friend brought me a video of **Prophet TB Joshua** praying. As I watched, something shifted inside me.

Tears streamed down my face as I began confessing my sins. I felt as though I had betrayed God. *Would He still love me?* I thought.

But my friend told me, *"Jesus still loves you, no matter what you've done."*

At that moment, I felt a **peace** I hadn't known in years. A peace that surpassed all understanding.

From Running to Redemption

For years, I had avoided church. If someone invited me, I would block them. I despised Christians because my abusive adopted mother claimed to be one.

But God wasn't done with me.

One day, I was walking in a Walgreens parking lot when a woman approached me and said, *"Can I provoke you?"*

Curious, I said, *"Yes."*

She invited me to church. I hesitated, but something inside me told me to go.

That Sunday morning, I did everything possible to miss the service. I stayed up late, watched movies, and convinced myself I wouldn't make it.

But at **6 AM**, a loud voice woke me up.

"Laura, get up and get ready for church!"

I ignored it and went back to sleep. But it came again. And again. By the third time, I felt something physically lifting me off the bed.

I obeyed.

I put on a white outfit—the only thing I had that seemed appropriate.

And when I walked into that church, I felt the **presence of God** in a way I never had before. I knew then—**this was home.**

This is just the beginning of my story. A journey from **brokenness to healing, from rejection to redemption**. If you're reading this, it's not by accident. There is a message here for you.

You are loved. You have a purpose. And your story isn't over yet.

Let me know if you'd like more refinements! I want to help you make this book as powerful and life-changing as possible.

Great! Below is a revised version of your testimony with improved structure, grammar, and readability while maintaining your original voice and message.

A Life Transformed by the Power of God

Falling in love with the things of God became second nature to me, but at the time, I didn't fully understand why. I could feel the fire of God in the church, and I said to myself, *I don't know what's really going on here, but whatever it is, I like it—and I want it.*

There was a sister sitting next to me, and I reached over, whispering, *How do you do that thing?*

She looked at me, confused. *What thing?*

The thing you were doing—your mouth moving, your body shaking. I want to do that too.

She smiled and explained, *It's not something you explain, but something you experience one-on-one.*

Determined, I told her, *Well, I want to experience it too.*

She had been speaking in tongues, and I longed for that same encounter with God.

The Day Everything Changed

The next time I went to church, I was especially excited because it was finally my baptism day. It was May 29th at 5 PM—I remember it as though it were yesterday. The message that day was powerful, and when the altar call came, I sat in my seat, hesitant. Yet, I could feel the presence of God so strongly.

As I sat there, I heard a voice speak to me, whispering in my ear: *Do you remember that thing you said you wanted? If you go up there, you will receive it.*

I was shocked. *Really?* I asked.

Yes, the voice responded.

Without hesitation, I got up so fast, as if something were pulling me toward the altar. At first, I stood there, looking around at everyone, unsure of what to do—like many first-timers. But then, the pastor urged us, *Come on! Don't just stand there looking at me. Say something to God! Praise Him! Give Him thanks!*

I didn't know exactly what to say, so I chose one word—*Hallelujah!* I repeated it over and over until I closed my eyes, shutting out distractions. I kept saying *Hallelujah* until suddenly, I felt my lips shaking, then my entire body trembling.

From that moment, I don't remember what happened next. All I know is that when I came back to myself, my sisters in Christ told me that five people had been holding me at once. I was shocked—*As small as I was, five people were holding me?!* But God works in mysterious ways.

Later that same day, I was baptized in water. I felt as light as a feather, and I couldn't stop talking about Jesus. My sisters in Christ laughed, saying they had the same experience after their baptism—the joy of the Lord was overwhelming!

A Life Forever Changed

After receiving the baptism of the Holy Spirit, followed by water baptism, my life was never the same. My way of thinking changed. My attitude transformed for the better. Most importantly, the Lord began to use me to touch and change lives through prayer, fasting, This is powerful and heartfelt! I can feel the depth of your experiences and the strength of your faith throughout your testimony. Below is a refined version that improves readability while keeping your passion and message intact.

Overcoming Pain Through the Power of Forgiveness and Faith

There are times in life when we have to ask God for the strength to forgive—especially when the pain is overwhelming and the hurt feels unbearable. It's never easy to experience betrayal or rejection from those you love. My God, it's painful! That's when Matthew 5:44 becomes so important:

"But I say unto you, Love your enemies, bless them that curse you, do good to them that hate you, and pray for them which despitefully use you and persecute you."

Most of us, in our pain, want to do the opposite. It's hard to love when you're hurting. But I can say this: it's not easy on your own, but with God inside of you, forgiveness becomes possible. When you are fully submitted to God, offenses and unforgiveness no longer have the same power over you. Of course, I'm not saying it's easy, but with the Holy Spirit, it can become easier.

All that I have been through has made me a stronger woman today. Though the journey hasn't been easy, I've learned that pain can either make you fall or cause you to rise. The key is to shift your focus from the past to the present and the future. Instead of carrying pain, bury it—bury it by choosing to forgive and move forward.

Think about it: If there was no hurt, there would be no need for healing. If there was no sickness, we wouldn't need a physician. If there was no hell, there wouldn't be a need for heaven. If there were no criminals, there would be no aneed for police, prisons, or justice systems. Everything in life serves a purpose—including pain.

When I first experienced deep hurt, I thought it was unfair and cruel. But as I look back, I see that my pain led me to God. It helped me find forgiveness, love, and humility. Sometimes, what seems like a crushing moment is actually the beginning of a breakthrough. What the enemy meant for evil, God always turns around for good.

I allowed myself to receive healing, and I let God transform my pain into purpose. When I was living in sin, I never imagined that one day I would be in church, praising and glorifying God. I used to run from the church, but now *I am the church.*

God's Protection Over My Life

I believe we must experience both good and evil so that when we see good, we can choose it and reject the evil. God doesn't make mistakes. As much as I once felt like my mother made a mistake by giving me away to be raised by another, I now see that it was all part of God's divine plan. He knew a day would come when I would turn to Him. He didn't need to prove anything—He simply waited, knowing I was coming.

Looking back, I realize how many times I could have died.

- **The Car Accident in Jamaica**: I was on my way to a football match when our car crashed into a bus. The impact was on my passenger side, and the bus was destroyed—but I walked away without a single scratch.
- **The Nightclub Shooting**: Years ago, when I was still partying, a shootout broke out inside the club. Bullets were flying everywhere, yet God protected me from death.
- **Two Car Accidents in One Week**: I survived not just one, but two accidents in the same week. Again, I walked away unharmed.

So many times, I could have lost my life, but God had me in the palm of His hands. Isaiah 49:16 says:

"See, I have engraved you on the palms of my hands; your walls are ever before me."

When it's your time, it's your time. But when it's not, nothing can take you out. Romans 8:31 reminds us:

"If God be for us, who can be against us?"

And Isaiah 54:17 declares:

"No weapon formed against you shall prosper, and every tongue that rises against you in judgment you shall condemn."

God's love and protection are real. He goes to great lengths to show us how much He cares. When I thought my life was over, He showed up, gave me strength, and fought for me to be here today.

Spiritual Warfare and the Call of God

John 10:10 tells us:

"The thief comes only to steal and kill and destroy; I have come that they may have life, and have it to the full."

We have an unseen enemy who will do anything to stop us from fulfilling our God-given calling. He uses death, loss, separation, manipulation, rejection, miscommunication, fornication, anger, arrogance, offenses, and unforgiveness to either kill us or slow us down. That's why we must choose whom we will serve.

Matthew 22:14 says:

"Many are called, but few are chosen."

Ecclesiastes 9:11 reminds us:

"The race is not to the swift, nor the battle to the strong."

The battle we face is not against flesh and blood, but against spiritual forces of darkness (Ephesians 6:12). That's why the enemy fights so hard—he wants to eliminate us before we can walk in our destiny. If he can take you out early, he will. But I'm grateful that God has been with me every step of the way, ensuring that I live and not die to declare His works.

There were times I felt like my calling would never manifest. The enemy whispered lies, trying to convince me that I wasn't chosen. But I had to find my strength in God, press on, and remind myself of His promises. Just like David encouraged himself in the Lord, I had to look in the mirror and declare:

"Simone, you will make it. You will live to see the fulfillment of your destiny."

Discerning God's Voice Amid Deception

I've learned that not every word spoken over your life is from God. I remember attending a men's crusade where a minister—who later admitted to drinking rum the night before—prophesied over me, saying, *"God told me to tell you that you are an evangelist."*

I was immediately troubled. I knew what God had told me, and this was not it. Right then, I discerned the spirit of deception and confusion trying to work through this minister.

Moments later, an elder in the church—filled with the fire of God—approached me and said, *"God said to tell you that you are a Prophetess."* She then asked if I had ever heard that before. I smiled and said, *"Yes, people have told me, and God Himself has told me."*

That was my confirmation! I realized that the enemy often tries to plant doubt in the minds of God's chosen ones. That's why it's so important to know God's voice for yourself. Philippians 4:6 says:

"Be careful for nothing; but in everything by prayer and supplication with thanksgiving let your requests be made known unto God."

One wrong word spoken over your life can mislead you forever. But when you have a true relationship with God, you will recognize deception and stand firm in your calling.

Pressing On to the Finish Line

Life will throw punches. People will reject you, mock you, and look down on you. But I've learned that what people think doesn't matter—only what God says does.

I may not have had wealth, a big house, or a high-paying job, but God doesn't call the qualified—He qualifies the called.

Through it all, I give God glory. My pain became my gain. My scars became my stars. My mess became my message. My test became my testimony. The race became grace.

So I encourage you: **keep going.** Don't give up before your breakthrough. Stay still and know that He is God. Remember Job—he lost everything, but he never cursed God. And in the end, God honored him.

No matter what you face, remain thankful. Keep your praise. Never complain in the fire—because when it's over, you'll come out as pure gold.

To God be the glory! I'll refine your passage while maintaining your passionate tone and powerful message. Below is a more structured and polished version:

Nothing is Wasted in God's Hands

One of the most important lessons I've learned is to love people despite their flaws and imperfections. No one is without fault, and everyone has something in life that keeps them seeking God. Some things we view as a curse are actually blessings in disguise. God doesn't waste anything—so why should we? Even the bad can be used for good, just as God has demonstrated time and time again.

The problem with many of us is that we complain too much instead of using what we have. We focus on what's lacking instead of realizing that everything we need is already in our hands. Use your pain, your stubbornness, and even your scars for God's glory. If you can't learn to use what you have, how will you build the Kingdom of God? When the enemy tells you that you're nothing, fight back by proving that you have what it takes to build a house, a marriage, and a ministry. Show him that your mind is made up and nothing he does can change it.

Even stubbornness can be used for good! That same trait the enemy tried to use against you can be turned into determination to follow God's calling. Instead of letting it lead you into rebellion, let it drive you to stay committed to your faith. Everything within you—your character, your gifts, even your appearance—can be used for God's purpose.

A Divine Encounter

Let me share an experience that opened my eyes to how God truly doesn't waste anything.

One day, after school, I was waiting at the bus stop when a young man approached me, clearly interested. He offered me a ride home, and at first, I refused. But then, I heard a voice say, *"Take the ride; it's a blessing."*

I obeyed.

As we drove, the young man expected small talk, maybe something casual or worldly. Instead, I began to minister to him. I spoke about God's love, His purpose, and His word. Suddenly, the young man stopped talking to me and started talking directly to God. He was in awe, repeating, *"God! God! Is this how You're doing things now?"*

He then confessed that the night before, he had been praying for an answer from God. And now, here I was, delivering that very answer. He was stunned that God had used someone like me—a young woman, someone he initially approached for the wrong reasons—to speak into his life.

That day, I realized that God will use whatever He pleases to reach His people. He doesn't waste anything—not our words, not our appearance, not even a simple moment at a bus stop. If we remain in the Spirit and not in the flesh, if we stay focused on God and His word, we will always hear His voice.

Are You Listening?

Many of us complain that God isn't speaking to us, but the truth is, He's always speaking. The question is: *Are we listening?*

God doesn't think like us, so the way we expect Him to communicate is often not how He chooses to speak. Sometimes, He speaks through a song on the radio, a scripture we randomly open, a conversation with a friend, or even a movie we're watching. When your mind is truly on God, you'll begin to see Him everywhere and in everything. You won't have to search for Him—He is already with you.

That's why He tells us, *"Be still and know that I am God."* To be still means to stop, slow down, and listen. Meditate on His word day and night. Let prayer become your hobby. Let worship become your lifestyle. Let thanksgiving be your daily offering. A grateful heart always catches God's attention.

The Power of Praise

I've learned that there is power in praise. When we praise God, Heaven responds. That's why the enemy works so hard to keep us distracted and discouraged—because he knows that if we focus on worship, God will fight on our behalf.

Look at the great men and women in the Bible. Every time they chose to praise God in the midst of their trials, they gained victory over their enemies. While they were busy giving thanks, God was busy sending angels to fight for them.

Think about it—when Jesus commanded the storm to be still, it obeyed. If your situation isn't calm yet, maybe there's something in the storm that will make you stronger. Maybe there's something in that raging water that will prepare you for your next season.

Faith Over Fear

Faith is when you don't see a way, yet you trust God anyway. It's not about figuring out the "how"—it's about knowing *who* is in control. Isn't it amazing when you're in a situation where there seems to be no way out, and then—boom!—God makes a way? That's the power of faith.

Yet, many of us worry about things that aren't even our burden to carry. Jesus already paid the price, but as humans, we tend to pick up unnecessary burdens. The Apostle Paul said, *"I find then a law, that when I would do good, evil is present with me" (Romans 7:21).* This means that as long as we're trying to walk with God, the enemy will always try to distract us. But the bottom line is—*what will you choose?* Good or evil? Faith or fear? Worship or worry?

God gives us choices. He won't force us to serve Him or love Him, even though He has the power to do so. Instead, He gives us free will. We have the power to choose love over hate, forgiveness over grudges, faith over doubt.

Who Are You Allowing to Use You?

One of the greatest tragedies I've observed is how the people we love the most are often the ones who hurt us the deepest. With the same mouth that blesses, we also curse. Jealousy, envy, and hatred take root, and before we know it, we become like vipers, attacking our own.

But how can you say you love someone while secretly hoping for their downfall? How can you claim to love your brother or sister while betraying them, trying to destroy their dreams, and tearing down their character? Worse still, how can you say you love God while hating your own blood?

This kind of behavior is exactly how the enemy operates—deception masked as love. The devil never truly loves those he uses; he only seeks to steal, kill, and destroy. And if we allow him, he will use us against ourselves and those we claim to love.

So I ask you today:.

Who Will You Allow to Use You—God or the Enemy?

Will you let God use your life for His glory? Or will you allow the devil to use you to build his kingdom of darkness?

The choice is yours.

Will you enhance and build the Kingdom of Heaven by giving God complete authority and control over your life? Or will you hand over the key that God gave you to access heaven—either returning it to Him or, worse, giving it to the enemy to unlock destruction over your precious soul?

Matthew 5:20 states:

"Except your righteousness shall exceed the righteousness of the scribes and Pharisees, ye shall in no case enter the kingdom of heaven."

This means we must choose whom we will serve.

Matthew 13:45-48 further illustrates this choice:

"Again, the kingdom of heaven is like unto a merchant in search of fine pearls. Upon finding a single pearl of great value, he went and sold all that he had and bought it. Again, the kingdom of heaven is like a dragnet, which was lowered into the sea and gathered fish of every kind. When it was full, they dragged it up on the beach and sat down and sorted out the good fish into baskets, but the worthless ones they threw away."

Take time to meditate on this. Do not be among the worthless ones—be useful to the Kingdom of Heaven. Do not allow the devil to use you ruthlessly.

My Journey of Faith

My journey began quickly after I got saved. God has used me in many ways—not only in my own life but also in the lives of others. Looking back, I am grateful that I answered the call. Let me share how God has used me to impact His people.

One day, while praying and fasting at home, I heard a name whispered to me. It was a name I had never heard before. God spoke to me about a young lady named Kam. He told me that she was going through a difficult time, feeling depressed, and in desperate need of someone to talk to. She was contemplating taking her own life.

God gave me her name and instructed me to call her and pray for her. In obedience, I asked for her phone number and reached out. Kam was surprised to receive a call from someone she had never met, but I explained who I was and why I was calling. As I spoke, she was deeply touched.

I prophesied to her, and she confirmed that everything I said was true—exactly what she was experiencing. She admitted that she had no one to talk to about her troubles. I reassured her, "Don't worry, God remembers you."

I prayed for her over the phone, and she said she felt the anointing and healing power of God setting her free from captivity. She thanked me, but I reminded her, "To God be the glory." She then asked if she could call me whenever she felt troubled or needed prayer. I agreed. From that moment on, she would call me from time to time, and I continued praying with her until she was completely set free from the occultic powers that had been tormenting her.

Kam had been feeling alone, rejected, and overlooked—even inside the church. No one wanted to be her friend. But despite her struggles, God had not forgotten her. He sent help, healing, and deliverance. I am grateful that I was able to be a friend to her when no one else in the church would.

Sadly, this is a common issue in the church today. Many people feel unloved, even though the church is supposed to be built on a foundation of love. We should embrace our brothers and sisters so they do not feel the need to search for love in the wrong places.

It was so bad that when I called Kam without her calling me first, she was shocked. No one from the church ever reached out to her or made time for her. Sometimes, we need to set aside time for others beyond ourselves and our families. While we are busy helping someone else, God is busy fixing the things that concern us.

Serving is not just about tithing, giving offerings, or assisting the pastor. It is also about taking time to pray for someone who desperately needs it. Fasting is not just for seeking personal breakthroughs—it is also for interceding on behalf of others who are struggling.

James 5:16 reminds us:

"Pray one for another."

Prayer is one of the most wonderful gifts you can give to someone—it is both a blessing for them and a blessing for you.

A Divine Encounter in the Barbershop

God moved again when He spoke to me in a barbershop one day. I was waiting for my brother to finish his haircut when I noticed a young man sitting in the back, talking to himself. At first, I thought it was strange, but as I observed him closely, I realized he was speaking to unseen spirits. He was waving his hands as if slapping them away and telling them to leave him alone.

A burden for him grew in my spirit. As I sat there, I prayed silently, "God, I wish this young man's life could change." I immediately heard God respond, "It can."

A pastor then walked into the barbershop to get his haircut. The burden in my heart was so strong that I asked him, "Pastor, can you pray for that young man?" He quickly replied, "Me? No, I won't touch that case unless God tells me to."

Everyone in the shop laughed. They thought the situation was too scary. But my spirit would not rest.

Then, God spoke to me: "Why don't you pray for him? Don't you know I have given you the power to set the captives free?"

I was taken aback. "Me?" I asked.

"Yes, you!" God affirmed.

This was my first encounter of this kind. I had prayed for people before, but never in a situation like this. Honestly, I was both shocked and a little afraid. But I knew I had to be obedient.

I walked over to the young man. He looked at me as if seeing something unfamiliar. I asked him, "May I pray with you?" To my surprise, he quickly said, "Yes!"—as if he was desperate for relief.

I laid hands on him and prayed with all my heart:

*"In the name y different—clean, healthy, and whole. No longer tormented, he was now working and living a normal life!

What an awesome God! He is a good, good Father.

Here's a structured and polished version of your passage with improved grammar, flow, and readability:

Then, his wife became pregnant and gave birth to twins—one boy and one girl. What an awesome God! What initially seemed broken and hopeless turned into someone's breakthrough moment. To God be all the glory!

After that, my assignment there was over, and I moved to another apartment nearby, where I got a job. It was manageable for the time being, and my daily routine consisted of work, church, and home. I rarely did anything else because I spent most of my time praying or studying the Word of God.

In this new place, I was the only one who was saved. I looked around and thought to myself, How can I make a difference here? How can I help lead some of these people to salvation? I knew this was my next assignment, so instead of complaining, I did what I do best—praying and fasting.

At first, they mocked my clothes and constant prayers, unaware that I was praying for them. But I didn't mind because I understood that they didn't know any better. From time to time, I ministered to them when the opportunity arose. However, I found that my actions spoke louder than my words. I continued living a life of holiness before them while praying fervently.

Eventually, they started asking me questions about my life—what I did and how I did it. I answered with grace and humility, and over time, they began to see that what the Word of God said made sense. Two out of three of them gave their lives to Christ, stopped their bad habits, and even started attending church. One of them also got married. Seeing the hand of God at work once again filled me with joy.

However, the third person did not get saved. Instead, they gave me notice to move out. I didn't argue. I simply said, "Okay," and left.

I then moved in with a friend who lived with her father and brother. Another assignment. But God was still moving. As usual, I let my life be a testimony and ministered when the opportunity arose.

Matthew 5:16 says, Let your light so shine before men, that they may see your good works and glorify your Father who is in heaven. I held on to that scripture and continued praying for them.

The young lady eventually went to church and was filled with the Holy Spirit—thank God! But her father and brother refused to listen to God's voice, and they paid the ultimate price for their disobedience.

The father constantly told me I needed God when, in reality, he was the one who needed God. I made it clear to him that I already had a relationship with Jesus and encouraged him to surrender his life to Christ. But instead of heeding my words, he chose to argue with me every chance he got.

Eventually, he went to sleep one night and never woke up. He had died without ever giving his life to God. It was heartbreaking.

His son, on the other hand, lived a reckless life—constantly in and out of trouble with the police, doing drugs, partying, and chasing women. I could give him the Word of God, but I couldn't force him to accept it. The choice was his. And the saddest thing is when people reject salvation and willingly choose destruction over Jesus Christ. Watching a soul perish is never easy.

Meanwhile, the daughter was diagnosed with brain cancer and suffered from excruciating pain. But I was grateful that she had surrendered her life to Jesus and chosen eternal life, even though the others did not.

In life, we all have a choice—life or death, the narrow road or the broad road. There is no in-between. It's either God or Satan. That's it! God gives us free will, but He does not force us.

As I continued my journey, I moved into a one-room place with a lady from Liberia. It was a temporary arrangement, but I didn't like the environment at all. The atmosphere was heavy, and every day felt like a spiritual battle. It was the longest three months of my life.

There were so many dark spirits in that place, and I had to wrestle with them constantly. I now understand that it was meant to strengthen me spiritually. But I survived because, even though I walked through the valley of the shadow of death, God was with me.

Sometimes, a place may seem fine physically, but spiritually, it's a death trap. However, God will sometimes allow us to walk into such situations because He already knows we will come out victorious. He knows we will conquer. Some people ask, Why would God allow this? But let me tell you why:

1. To remind you that He is always with you and that you should not fear, no matter what things look like.

2. To help you discover the power of God within you.

Think about it—if there were no principalities, demons, or spiritual battles, there would be no need for prayer, spiritual growth, or the church. If there were no hell, there would be no need for heaven. Everything happens for a reason, a season, and a time.

Matthew 5:18 says, Heaven and earth will pass away, but not one jot or tittle shall in no wise pass from the law, till all be fulfilled.

God sometimes leads us into battles so that we can see His victory and understand the power we carry within us.

The time came for me to move again, but I had nowhere to go. I cried out to God for help. Then, my phone rang. It was a friend I had been inviting to church. I had previously shared my testimony with him, and he told me it had touched his heart.

He said he wanted me to take him to church on his birthday—the same day I was asked to leave. I thought to myself, What kind of sign is this? On his birthday, he wants to be in God's presence?

Even though I was dealing with my own situation, I decided to take him to church. I told the Liberian lady, "I'll leave my stuff here, but I'll come back for it." She agreed.

The church service was powerful, and by the end of the night, my friend gave his life to Christ! I was overjoyed to witness another soul saved.

But after the service, reality hit me—I had nowhere to go. Sitting in his car, I silently prayed, God, what do I do now?

He then asked me, "Where should I drop you off?"

I hesitated before answering, "I don't have a home to go to."

He was shocked. "Why didn't you tell me earlier?"

I told him I had been more focused on getting him to church.

He then said, "What if I had made other plans tonight?"

I replied, "Well, you asked."

Out of kindness, he took me to his house since he had an extra room. However, all my belongings were still at the Liberian lady's house, so I had nothing to change into. My birthday was only a few days away, and it was embarrassing to be without my things.

The next day, I reached out to the Liberian lady to ask if I could pick up my clothes. She refused, saying she wouldn't be home until Thursday—even though my birthday was on Wednesday.

I had no choice but to wear the same clothes for three days.

Finally, on Thursday, my friend took me to collect my belongings. I was relieved to have them back. But then, he told me his parents were coming, and I could no longer stay at his place.

I reached out to my sister, explaining my situation, and she said she would ask her husband.

At first, he said no.

I was heartbroken. A pastor refusing to help? I thought we were supposed to support each other.

But I didn't dwell on it. I took my burdens to God.

(...to be continued)

Edited Version:

I noticed that my sister and in-law started acting very differently toward me. They would go out without saying a word and sometimes stay out all night. At one point, they were gone for about three days. Then, I received a phone call from my sister while she was still away. I assumed she was checking on me, but instead, she asked, "Why are you doing what you're doing? You need to stop."

Confused, I asked, "Stop what? What are you talking about?"

She replied, "You need to stop working witchcraft on me because I was telling you off the other day, and the Lord told me you're working against me."

I was shocked. Me? Witchcraft? I couldn't believe what I was hearing. I said to her, "I don't know which voice is talking to you, but I know it's not God. He would never tell you something that isn't true, because He is not a man that He should lie."

At that moment, I realized confusion was at work, but I wasn't sure exactly what was going on. I began to wonder—had they taken a vacation without telling me? Why this sudden accusation? Normally, we communicated about our whereabouts for safety reasons. But now, something was clearly off.

I observed their behavior. They would see me in the house and not speak to me. As soon as they saw me coming, they would start yelling, supposedly praying and speaking in tongues. I felt like an outcast—rejected and hurt. They would shout things like, "We don't want no witch in here! In the name of Jesus, we can't be living with a witch! That witch must die!"

I knew they were talking about me, but instead of defending myself, I said, "Lord, You will fight my battles." Then, I remembered Matthew 5:10-11:

"Blessed are they which are persecuted for righteousness' sake: for theirs is the kingdom of heaven. Blessed are ye when men shall revile you, and persecute you, and shall say all manner of evil against you falsely, for my sake."

Wow! All I did was pray for them—for God's divine protection and blessings over their lives—and now, I was being accused of witchcraft? It was confusing, but I understood that persecution often follows righteousness.

I packed my things. My ride came, and I thanked my in-law. My sister then asked, "Are you going to be okay where you're going?"

I thought, How am I supposed to know that? This is my first time going there. And if you were so concerned, why did you kick me out?

I left for New York, trying to hope for the best. I arrived around 3:00 AM, trying to be as quiet as possible. My friend asked Lady M, the caretaker for his mother, if I could stay with her, but she refused. He then insisted I take his room while he slept in the living room. I was grateful.

The next day, we discussed my stay and how to make things work since the only available room was his. I didn't want to make him uncomfortable, but he insisted. From that point, I tried my best to adjust and not be too hard on myself.

I started looking for work again but had no luck. Still, I kept pushing, telling myself, Simone, you can't give up.

Not long after, I developed a persistent cough that became very uncomfortable for my throat. I tried home remedies like ginger tea, but nothing worked. I lost my appetite—I didn't want to eat anything; all I wanted was for the cough to go away, but it wouldn't.

People around me started asking if I was okay. I replied, "Not really, but I think I'll be fine." The caretaker, Lady M, said she thought it was stress. Then, she began asking if I was looking for jobs and offering suggestions.

I thought, Do people have no mercy or compassion anymore? After being kicked out by my own family, falsely accused of witchcraft, and now sick without knowing why, you're asking me about jobs?

It felt like all people cared about was money and work.

Lady M eventually asked what had happened and why I was there. I wasn't ashamed of the truth, so I told her. She was shocked and asked, "Are you sure you didn't do anything to them for them to kick you out like that?"

I knew what she was thinking—just like Job's friends assumed he must have sinned to deserve his suffering. But I said, "I didn't do anything wrong." I didn't bother defending myself because I knew they wouldn't believe me. But God is my defense. He always fights for the poor, the needy, the homeless, and the fatherless.

As more people visited the house, they, too, asked me why I was there. I grew tired of answering the same questions, especially since I barely had the strength to talk. I felt like a motherless child.

But I reminded myself: God, You know all things. Only You know why I'm in this situation. And for what it's worth, I know it's for something greater to come. So I will wait until my change comes.

Despite my worsening health, all people seemed to care about was material things. I was literally dying—ignored, misjudged, and seen as a girl with nowhere to go, as if I had no ambition. But life is more than ambition. Without life, you can't do anything at all.

After two weeks, my cough still hadn't stopped. One day, my body started shaking uncontrollably, and I felt an unbearable coldness. I knew something was seriously wrong.

I decided to visit the doctor, but people kept discouraging me, saying I shouldn't rush to the hospital. I tried to endure, but I only got worse. I became weak, bedridden, and unable to eat. Even a single slice of bread or a cup of tea felt impossible to finish.

Then, I heard a voice speak to me:

"Daughter, go to the hospital. Don't let anyone drive fear into you."

As soon as I heard that voice, something stirred in my spirit. I took a bold step and asked for a ride to the emergency room.

At the hospital, I saw people in worse conditions than mine—though I didn't yet know my situation was deadly. I waited as they checked my blood pressure and performed routine procedures. The emergency room was full that day, so I had to wait a long time. At one point, I grew discouraged.

Finally, a doctor came to my section. They ran tests, drew blood, and examined me.

Then came the moment of truth.

The doctor returned with the results.

"You have walking pneumonia," he said. Here's a structured and polished version of your passage with improved flow, grammar, and clarity while keeping the original emotions intact:

The doctor told me my condition was very rare for someone my age. He also noted that I was extremely lucky. When I asked why, he said, "If you had waited until tomorrow, you wouldn't have made it. You would have died."

Hearing those words sent chills through me. My oxygen levels had been dangerously low, but God was right on time. He never leaves or forsakes us. I couldn't help but think to myself, What an awesome God we serve! Just a few more hours, and I would have been gone, but God said, Not so! He showed up for me, and for that, I am eternally grateful. Even now, when I remember that moment, I still feel the emotions wash over me.

I was admitted to the hospital, where I spent seven days. I couldn't breathe on my own because my oxygen levels were critically low, so I had to use a breathing machine. Every day, I was pricked with needles as they carried out endless tests. At one point, the doctors told me seven different things were wrong with me simultaneously. My menstrual cycle had ceased, and nothing in my body was functioning as it should. It was as if I was already dead, with only my breath left to go. But even then, God was fighting for me.

God holds the keys to life and death. At that moment, I realized something profound—nothing is more important than your health and your life. If you don't have life, you have nothing. And if you don't have God, you have nothing. Without Him, we are like vapor in the wind. That experience taught me to appreciate my life more and to take better care of my health.

It wasn't as if I had been careless with my body, but being homeless, exposed to the elements, with nowhere to go and no one to turn to but God, had put me in that position. Through it all, I learned a hard truth: people can be incredibly selfish. In this life, it often feels like every man is for himself. It's rare to find people who genuinely care without some hidden agenda.

Lying in that hospital bed, unable to move, hooked up to IV drips and monitors, I experienced something I never had before—a near-death experience. I had heard people say they saw death coming for them, but now, I understood. I longed to see a familiar face, but none of my family came. The only ones who visited were my newfound friend and a few others

I barely knew. It was kind of them, but the absence of those who claimed to love me was a painful realization.

I wondered, Where is the mercy in human beings? The Bible says, "The heart of man is desperately wicked" (Jeremiah 17:9), and "Every inclination of the human heart is evil from childhood" (Genesis 6:5). I had always known these verses, but now, I had lived them. Strangers showed me more kindness than those I had known my whole life. Why is it like that? Are people blind to their own neglect, or do they just not care? We should all ask God to purge our hearts and create in us a new spirit, just as David did.

I wasn't surprised that my family never showed up, yet, somehow, I was. But I have come to accept that not everyone's destiny is the same.

During those seven days in the hospital, I met new people—nurses, doctors, patients from different backgrounds, cultures, and walks of life. When you are in a vulnerable situation, you realize that none of those things matter. People are just people, and we should love one another as we love ourselves. I was grateful for those who visited and for those who cared. And I thanked God, even for those who didn't. Because through it all, He never left my side. When the visitors came and went, He remained.

After many tests and treatments, I finally recovered. My body healed, my strength returned, and I could breathe on my own again. But as I prepared to leave the hospital, another worry weighed on me—I had nowhere to go. The place I had been staying wasn't guaranteed, and I didn't know if I could return.

Thankfully, my friend came to pick me up from the hospital and took me back to his parents' house. But even then, I knew his decision wasn't final. Others in the household—his siblings and his mother's caretaker—also had a say in who could stay. Most of his family were pastors and Christians, and the house had once belonged to their parents. His father had passed away, and his mother was now under someone else's care.

It was a lot to consider, but my friend made what I would call a bold faith move. He knew the decision wasn't entirely his, but he stepped out in faith anyway. Because the reality was—I needed somewhere to stay.

I arrived at the house still weak, still recovering, but filled with gratitude. When you've come so close to losing your life, you see things differently. You begin to recognize people for their hearts rather than their appearances. I had learned so much from my struggles, and though my journey wasn't over, one thing was certain—God had been with me every step of the way. Here's a structured and polished version of your passage with improved flow, grammar, and clarity while keeping the original emotions intact:

As I lay there, my life flashed before my eyes. I knew I could have been dead, but I wasn't. I had so much to thank God for.

I had a lot on my mind, but I believed I would get better, so I wasn't worried about that part. However, I was deeply concerned about being in such a vulnerable state—physically, emotionally, and even spiritually. I had many thoughts racing through my mind, but I prayed and left it all in God's hands.

I reached out to one of the brothers in charge of handling most of the house's affairs, as well as his sister, who made decisions for their mother and the household. After speaking to them, they agreed that I could stay for a while—at least until I fully recovered. I thanked them both and was genuinely grateful for their kindness.

The recovery process was slow and challenging. My body and immune system had been turned upside down. It felt as if I were a newborn baby, learning to walk, eat, and function all over again. But God is awesome in how He works. He heals us, strengthens us, and walks with us through every valley—even through the shadow of death.

With time and patience, I gradually regained my strength. As I continued to heal, I started looking for jobs because the pressure on me was intense. Recovering, finding a stable place to live, and securing a job—all at once—felt overwhelming. Getting a job so soon, when I wasn't even fully well, was a big risk, but I had no choice. The family had made it clear that my stay was temporary, so I searched for jobs like my life depended on it.

Some people advised me to take it slow because I wasn't fully healed yet. I knew they were right, but I didn't have the luxury of waiting. I wasn't in my own home, and I could feel the weight of being in someone else's space. That uncomfortable feeling of people constantly watching you, knowing you don't belong, is suffocating. The pressure was enough to push anyone into depression, and I wasn't an exception.

Even while taking my medication and attending my doctor's appointments, my mind wasn't at rest. I was still fragile, still healing, but I had so many worries. The experience made me realize how few true friends I had. I could count on one hand how many people checked on me, visited, or even called. No family—just a few newfound friends I now considered family. But through it all, the Lord was my strength.

One day, during a routine doctor's visit, something unexpected happened. As I sat in the waiting area, I saw a woman coming from the doctor's office. Our eyes met, and something about that moment felt different. She walked over to me and asked, "Are you Jamaican?"

I replied, "Yes."

Instantly, she took a liking to me. I didn't know why, but I call it grace. Though she wasn't a doctor, she was willing to help me navigate the process at the doctor's office. We talked for a while, sharing a little about ourselves. Then, she gave me her phone number and told me I could reach out to her anytime.

I was moved. Here was a complete stranger, yet she was willing to help me so much—more than some of the people I had known for years. I call that favor. As we sat together, she browsed the web, looking for programs that could help my situation. Though she didn't find much, we came across something that had the potential to change my life forever—a school program. She took it upon herself to do everything necessary to get me enrolled, and by the grace of God, I got in.

I was beyond grateful. I had always wanted to go to school, but I never had the money. Education can be expensive, especially without financial support. So, I saw this as nothing short of a divine opportunity. I started with a summer program, and from that moment, my journey as a student began.

School helped take my mind off many of my worries, but from time to time, reality hit me—I still had nowhere to go. The family I was staying with made it clear that I was not welcome for much longer. I understood that they weren't my family, so it wasn't their responsibility to take me in, but as fellow believers in Christ, I had hoped for more compassion. Unfortunately, that wasn't the case.

Every day, I thought about my situation. I knew my days in that house were numbered, but I didn't know where I would go next. It wasn't funny. It wasn't easy. But I lived each day by faith, trusting that God would make a way.

The pressure in the house was overwhelming. Sometimes, I had to hide just to avoid another conversation about when I was leaving. I knew that every time I ran into them, they would ask, "When are you moving?" Even when I told them I was attending school, their response was, "But when are you moving? You need to find a job."

One of the women in the house suggested that I take a housekeeping or babysitting job. I thought to myself, Imagine, I finally have the chance to go to school, and you're telling me to get a housekeeping job—as if I'm not good enough to be educated. Her own children had gone to school, and some were still attending. I knew she would never expect them to settle for housekeeping jobs. So why did she think it was okay for me?

I understood that she didn't care about my future because I wasn't her family. But where was the love of God?

I told her I wasn't interested—I was going to school. She asked, "But how will you get a job in that field when you finish?"

I simply replied, "God will do it for me."

She sighed and said, "Okay." But then she added, "You need to find somewhere to go because you have to leave soon."

I knew the pressure was too much, but deep down, I had already decided—I wouldn't let anyone stop me from finishing my education. Even if they threw me out, I didn't care. It wouldn't be the first time. I had to protect my future, no matter what. This was a prophetic opportunity, and I couldn't afford to miss it. God would fight my battle.

One of the family's sisters came to visit from Florida. When she saw me, she assumed I was involved with her brother. She quickly pulled me aside and said, "Let me give you some advice."

I listened as she continued, "First, you're not a part of our family, and you don't belong here. Second, my brother is not good for you—I don't want to see you end up in that back room. That's not progress for a young girl like you."

I laughed to myself, thinking, Why does she assume I'm interested in her brother? Maybe because I was staying in their house, they felt entitled to bombard me with questions and suspicions.

I was stunned. These were Christians. Yet, there was no love. Then they wonder why people don't listen to them when they preach!

That day, her words hit me like a bullet. Imagine if I had been weak—I might have ended my life right then and there. Some people don't realize the weight their words carry. Love, love, love—that is what the church should be about.

But I have to say this: Many pastors will not make it to heaven. No matter how much they preach or pray, if they don't get it right with God and truly love others, they will fail the test. There is no love!

Where is the love in the church? Where is the church?

Her words hurt me deeply. No one in my state of mind needed to be reminded that they don't belong. It was cold and heartless. I pray that the Lord gives her understanding because true Christianity isn't just about words—it's about love in action.

This version keeps your story powerful while making it clearer, smoother, and more impactful. Let me know if you need any changes!

This passage is powerful and deeply personal, but it needs some restructuring and grammatical refinement to enhance clarity, engagement, and flow. Below is a more structured and polished version while keeping your authentic voice intact.

Faith Through Fire: A Journey of Trials and Triumph

God's ways are not our ways, and His thoughts are beyond our understanding. If this had been my one chance to make it to heaven, I would have missed it—but thank God it wasn't. My God!

I found myself wondering: Where is the love? Where is the faith? It seemed to have suddenly disappeared.

One day, my sister finally called me. After kicking me out and never checking on me—not even when I was in the hospital, where I could have died if not for the grace of God—she decided to check in. But God! He brought me through it all.

As we spoke, I told her I was healing well. She shared that she had found a job, and I expressed my happiness for her. But after that call, I tried reaching out to her again and realized her number was no longer working. I wondered what was going on. Was she okay? I had forgiven her and held nothing in my heart against her or her husband, yet something felt off.

Later, when my mother called to check on me, she mentioned she had heard I wasn't doing too well. I assured her that, by God's grace, I was healing. However, because I was worried about my sister, I asked my mother if she had heard from her. That's when she told me that my sister had changed her number.

I was shocked. Why would she change her number and not tell me? What had I done? I searched my spirit for answers, talking to God, asking, Why? What happened?

Then, not too long after, God answered me through my mother. She told me my sister had accused me of working witchcraft against her and her husband, even going so far as to claim that I was trying to take her husband from her.

I was stunned.

After kicking me out, was that still not enough? Now, she had to spread lies about me, turning people against me, giving me enemies I never asked for. I sat in disbelief, thinking, You can never truly understand human beings. No matter how hard you try, no matter how much you think you know them, you don't.

Was this how much my own sister hated me? After all the love I had shown her? After all the prayers I had prayed for her, with nothing but love in my heart? Wow.

Then, I remembered the scripture in Matthew 5:10: Blessed are those who are persecuted for righteousness' sake, for theirs is the kingdom of heaven.

My good was being spoken of as evil, but I refused to worry. I understood that grace wins every time. Still, it hurt to know that the ones you love the most are often the very ones who cause you the most pain.

I counted my loss, surrendered it to God, and forgave.

Nowhere to Go but God

As time passed, my eviction deadline loomed closer. My sister had blocked me, changed her number, and cut all ties with me. The people I was staying with were now forcing me out.

I had nowhere to go.

No family.

No job.

No papers.

No safety net.

All I had was God. And only He could save and deliver me.

I finished my summer classes, excited for the next semester, but I still had no place to stay. It was rough. Christians—those who should have shown mercy—showed none when I needed it most. But I stayed on my knees, fighting it out in prayer.

And then, just like God sent Jonathan to David, He sent someone into my life to help me. Because of them, I was able to find a place when I was kicked out.

Still, I couldn't help but wonder—how do these people sleep at night? Those who claim to love God yet leave the needy stranded? Do they have no conscience?

I believe in Galatians 6:7: Whatever a man sows, that he will also reap.

If I had turned my back on someone in need, I wouldn't be able to sleep. My spirit would have been tormented. But not everyone carries the same grace, and I had to learn to accept that.

God made a way. Here's a more polished and structured version of your passage. I've preserved your message while improving readability, grammar, and flow.

Embracing Your Calling and Overcoming Unforgiveness

It's hard for others to fully understand me. I often feel like I'm one of a kind—there's no duplicate or second version of me. The things I endure on a daily basis would break most people my age. A prison experience, for example, can destroy one part of you, yet at the same time, bring out greatness.

When you've been through a lot in life, it fuels a determination to achieve great things. But this journey has two sides: it can strengthen you, but it can also make you doubt yourself, struggle with low self-esteem, or feel like you're never good enough. You wrestle with your personality, striving for success, yet feeling crushed by past wounds. However, true healing comes from Yah.

After being crushed, squeezed, and broken, healing begins with the renewing of your mind. The key to overcoming hate is forgiveness. But how do you forgive when the pain is still fresh? How do you conquer bitterness and open your heart to love again?

It's a process—one that starts with prayer and fasting. Ask Yah to help you release the pain and offenses. When you do, God will enter your heart and heal those wounds. He will reveal to you that the person who hurt you was not acting alone—it was the spirit within them that caused the harm. When you understand this, true forgiveness becomes possible.

Forgiving someone is not just for their benefit—it's for yours. By refusing to forgive, you unknowingly keep yourself trapped, blocking your own blessings, joy, and spiritual growth. Yah commands us to forgive because He, too, is merciful. Imagine asking for His forgiveness, only for Him to say no. How would that feel? If we want to be forgiven, we must also extend forgiveness to others.

Jesus said to forgive "seventy times seven," meaning there should be no limit to our forgiveness. And when He referred to "your brother," He didn't just mean a biological sibling—He meant your spouse, your neighbor, your friend, your pastor. Too often, people avoid forgiveness by making excuses. Some even leave churches, states, or entire communities just to escape a person they refuse to forgive. But you can't hide from God—He sees your heart. True wisdom is found in forgiveness, not avoidance.

On Judgment Day, we will each stand alone before God, accountable for our actions. If He asks why we never forgave, what will our answer be? Pain is real, and hurt cuts deep, but God has given us the tools to overcome. Follow the steps I've laid out, and you'll find that forgiveness is possible. Philippians

4:13 says, "I can do all things through Christ who strengthens me." That includes forgiveness.

Walking in Your Calling

Many people complain that their lives aren't going the way they want. They feel stuck, unfulfilled, and frustrated. But have you ever considered that the reason you're struggling might be because you're running from your calling?

God has a plan for each of us. The package He has prepared for you—your blessings, opportunities, and purpose—is waiting. But if you don't step into your calling, you can miss out on everything that's meant for you.

I've seen people take job after job, trying different things, yet nothing works out. Why? Because they are not walking in their God-given purpose. Some even defend their choices, insisting, "That's not my calling." But deep down, they know the truth—they just don't want to face it.

Running from your calling won't lead to peace; it will only bring more struggles. If you already know your calling and refuse to walk in it, you will face the consequences. Even if you don't yet know your calling, but God sends someone to reveal it to you and you still reject it, you will still face challenges. Many say, "God didn't tell me that." But what if He sent a messenger to speak on His behalf?

The issue is not whether God has spoken—the issue is disobedience. And disobedience comes with consequences. The Bible says, "Obedience is better than sacrifice" (1 Samuel 15:22). You might think you're outsmarting God by ignoring His calling, but in reality, you're only fooling yourself.

When you accept your calling, you experience true peace. Your calling is not just about you—it's about the people connected to your obedience. When you step into your purpose, you open doors for others to encounter God.

If you continue to resist, you might experience turbulence in your life—just like Jonah. When Jonah tried to flee from God's assignment, the Lord sent a storm to shake him. If you are facing constant struggles, ask yourself: Is my disobedience the cause?

The good news is, you can still fix it. Repent, embrace your calling, and move forward in peace. The reality is, you cannot escape God. There is nowhere to hide from Him. Instead of running, surrender to His will. It may not be easy, but it will be worth it.

Your calling is a divine package, filled with everything you need—provision, fulfillment, and peace. Choosing to run from it only leads to suffering, but embracing it leads to a life of purpose.

So, ask yourself: Are you truly happy? Are you walking in your calling? The choice is yours—continue running or step into the life God has designed for you.

Your calling is your blessing. Accept it, embrace it, and let Yah use you for His glory.

This version keeps your message powerful while making it more readable. Let me know if you'd like any changes! Here is a refined version of your story, broken into clear paragraphs and polished for readability while preserving its powerful message:

God's Wrath and the Importance of Fearing Him

Grace—God's grace will keep and carry you. He will never leave you; He's with you all the way to the end. But let's talk about something we often forget: God's wrath. I don't understand why some people aren't afraid of God's wrath when, in fact, we should be. He is the only one we should fear because He has the power to give life and take life. Yet, strangely enough, many of us aren't aware of or afraid of God's wrath. But the fear of God is the beginning of wisdom, and we need this fear. When you don't fear God, you live as if you can do whatever you want without consequences. But one thing is certain: you won't get away with it. God sees everything—nothing escapes His notice—and He is to be feared because we do not want to incur His wrath.

Some people even go as far as denying God's existence, believing that everything they achieve is by their own strength or ability. If that's you, I urge you to stop and think again. Remember King Nebuchadnezzar, the most powerful of all the Babylonian kings. When you read the story about him, you will understand why I talk about the wrath of God. No matter how powerful you are, there's always someone greater. Power belongs to God alone—He is the ultimate source of all power and greatness. But when you forget this and act as if power doesn't come from God, you risk invoking His wrath.

God gives life, and He can take it away. He makes rich and poor. Yes, He even kills. Read it yourself in 1 Samuel 2:6. That's why we must fear God—so we don't incur His wrath upon ourselves or our descendants.

I have witnessed God's wrath firsthand. I was assigned to pray for a man in my church, someone who came from a rough background. God knew I could handle the assignment, so He gave it to me. I prayed and fasted for him, and in the spirit realm, God used me to break the chains that had him bound. He was spiritually shackled to the point that he couldn't move. When I saw that, I knew for sure that principalities and powers are real. There are wicked people on this earth.

After completing the assignment, I received a word from the Lord for him, along with some instructions and warnings regarding how he was living his life. Though I can't go into detail, I told him that he was on the wrong path and that God had warned him. Unfortunately, he didn't take the warning seriously. He continued down the same destructive path, ignoring God's voice.

God told me that if he didn't change, he would experience His wrath. Sadly, I witnessed the consequences. This man lost everything he had—including his sanity. When I saw him next, I could hardly believe the transformation. His disobedience had triggered God's wrath, and the results were devastating. It was heartbreaking, and I begged God for mercy on his behalf. But God had warned him, and now the wrath was inevitable.

This experience made me even more afraid of God. When God is serious, He is serious. King Nebuchadnezzar was once a mighty king, but when he acted as though power didn't belong to God, he incurred God's wrath. The result?

He was driven from men, eating grass like an ox, his hair grew like eagle's feathers, and his nails like bird claws. Think about that. And still, there are people who refuse to fear God. They forget that He is both a loving and a dreadful God—a God mighty in battle, awesome in power.

Psalm 99:3 says, "Let them praise your great and awesome name—He is holy." Don't think you can play with God and get away with it. Don't think too highly of yourself as if God can't see you wherever you are. He is faithful, but He is also a God to be feared. You might think you can escape the consequences of rebellious actions, but you can't. It's only a matter of time before God's judgment comes.

God gives us many chances to repent because He doesn't want to destroy us. He doesn't want us to end up in the lake of fire, but when we act as though we can challenge our Maker, we force God to pour out His wrath. That's what we want to avoid. If you don't understand God's wrath, read the book of Revelation by John the Revelator. All who knew God feared Him. If you truly understand who God is, you would fear Him too.

My advice is this: fear God and live your life carefully, for He is watching you. Sometimes we should learn to act like children toward our Heavenly Father, because He is our Father. Fathers don't like it when their children misbehave or disobey them. I know my father was happy when I listened and followed his instructions without arguing. That's exactly what our Heavenly Father is looking for—obedience. We shouldn't act as though we don't need our Father. We need Him more than we think, in every step we take and in everything we do.

When I say "be childlike," I don't mean that you should act like a five-year-old when you're an adult. To be childlike with God means to trust Him, let go, and rest in His arms. Be obedient and have faith without complaining. Don't worry about things that are beyond your control. Leave them for God to handle. Some things are clearly not ours to handle but His. That's what it means to be childlike. Just as a child runs to their father when they need help, we should run to our Heavenly Father with honesty, knowing He sees and knows everything.

As a child, I was always obedient to my parents. I may have had a few moments when I wanted to do my own thing, but for the most part, I listened. There was one thing I remember, though: my parents were both smokers, and they would send me to buy cigarettes for them. In the islands, children could go to the shops and buy things like cigarettes in small amounts—often just a few sticks.

One day, I went to buy cigarettes for my mother, and I was approached by a man who ran the shop. He offered me candy, which I took. But soon after, he lured me into his house, where he assaulted me. I was just a small child—around five years old—yet the enemy was already trying to destroy me. He threatened me not to tell anyone. At that young age, I didn't fully understand what was happening, but I knew something was wrong.

This man wasn't the only one. Another time, I went to a different shop, and again, I was confronted by another predator. Thankfully, I was able to run away and escape, but the trauma stayed with me. The enemy doesn't stop. He will use any means possible to destroy you from a young age.

But God protected me. Eventually, I moved in with my adopted mother, who was a Christian and didn't drink or smoke. I thought I was safe, but the enemy's attacks didn't stop. Even when I thought I was in a better environment, the enemy was still after me. But I thank God for His protection, even when I didn't fully understand it.I was not ! **Safe,** ***so it started with a friend of hers that use to visit her very often and at times he use to sleep over at her house the guy in question was more like a son to her and i believed she loved him like a son, but does not live with us it was just the two of us in our six bedroom house so from time to time he sleep over so he was more like a family friend and trusted by my mother so no one was suspecting him of anything funny, i use to be around him when he fixing stuff around the house and it was harmless to me at the time he gained my trust and everybody else's trust so no one knew he would be a child molester or pedophile it look far from him you couldn't tell by his behavior but you can never tell.One day my mom went out and because he was trusted family friend she left me at home with him, i was doing my house chores and he was in bed when she was leaving i believe i was sweeping the house like i do every morning when i got to his room i knocked he said i should***

come in, and like i said he was trusted i went in to clean his room also he interrupted me with my cleaning and pull me to his bed i was a child and wasn't too sure what was going on he pull of my undies and was looking at my private, touching it, and put his mouth on it, his fingers trying to pave the way for his private i guess, so at that point i was still wondering what's going on even though it wasn't the first time i would be molested by older men that could be my father two times, i didn't say anything and to be honest i don't remember if i was told not to say anything but i didn't say anything and my little undies was pull down so many times maybe to me it was normal, because people kept on abusing me and even my mom use to ask me to pull off my undies so she can search me, so at this point it seems normal i guess if every-time your undies been pull down and touch or ask you to pull it off, my abusers use to pull of my undies on their own but my mom use to ask me to pull it down to search me, so at this point like i said it seems normal i didn't really get it but i know i was uncomfortable each time my undies was pulled down or ask to pull down.by the time i got in my teens i was mentally abused and traumatized by predators and sex offenders and abusers and sometimes i use to sit down and tears would just ran out of eyes my mom use to ask me why i'm crying and i use to say nothing or i don't know and she use to asked me how come you crying and you don't have any reasons why stop crying before i give you something to cry for but i didn't even know why i was crying or i wasn't sure why but i know it's hurt but can't identify which one or by who each time so i use to just have these random burst out of tears without being able to identify exactly why i just knew i was not happy that's all, and to round it all off i call this one the grand finale because it was the last i was abused but this time it was rape and it was when i was fifteen years old, when got raped with a gun to my face and i was told if i say anything i will die, it was the last time and the number of times i was violated was eight times in number after all that i was broken down and the definition of traumatized and very suicidal and tried taking my life a few times but God didn't allow it happen i struggle with my emotions and the voices in my head i was a disturb young woman who been through hell and back but though i had so much going on in my life i never show it on the outside it doesn't look like what have been through, but God.after all that i developed hate towards men i thought they were all the same at one point and didn't want to have anything to do with them i

thought i should just get my pound of flesh on them because i thought they were wicked.I can remember i didn't want to have anything to do with them and when i do it was not nice and i was not nice with them either, after so many episodes of hurt and pain i didn't think there was anything left for me to experience or go through i thought that was it for me with hurt and pain, so i moved on with my life but honestly inside i was hurting and wounded by pain so much pain and hurt but i still manage to think i was fine.I got married at twenty years old and start a family i thought i knew what i was doing and like i said i thought i was fine, after getting married i still went through hell in my marriage as a young couple i can't say i was perfect, but i knew i did my best as a young wife but my best was still not good enough, the enemy came back at me through my husband again, even thought i was married my husband treated me like a prostitute and with so much rejection it was as if i wasn't even married so i was married but still alone when i thought my problems was over it just started i became very depressed in my marriage to the point i wasn't eating well and was loosing so much weight i was skinny the marriage was draining me and put me in depression, so it didn't last for long after dealing with a constant cheating husband and a husband that your rejected by you have no choice than to leave before you die of depression, i left my husband's house and was battling with depression so started drinking thinking that drinking would take away my troubles, i started drinking to the point drinking became my best friend i use to have a few friends i hand out with but when they see me they always cheer up because they thought i was funny and the life of the party, but what friends didn't know is that i was battling with depression i use go out at nights with my friends drink my sorrow away but except they never went away sometimes i come home and when i get home i use sit down and cry and drink even more until i feel like i want to sleep, so come home cry drink myself to sleep and wake the next day and do the same thing again, for about three to four years i stayed in depression and wallow in my pains.I started taking up music and that's kind of somewhat help because i started writing and rapping and singing and so when i do i believe it was helping me but not totally i was still disturbed by my troubled pass and my pains but i was a bit better than before.I started on a journey that was not so wonderful either, i was still suffering from depression at times i would be happy and then next moment i get so lost in thoughts spaced out in a

trance thinking and sudden emotions of sudden sadness, it was very bad i knew at this point i needed help but to be honest with you the only help i needed was Jesus, i knew i was on to something but don't know exactly what i'm onto, i was seeing a psychiatrist at one point but i don't think it was helping at all i was still messed up i was still depressed until i tried to kill myself again it was bad, i knew something was terribly wrong with me, and the only solution came across was Jesus, yes Jesus did in my life what the doctor's and psychiatrist couldn't do, deliver my soul from that depression i was battling, i prayed i told God i was tired of the way my life was and he answered me, i open up my heart and let flesh on them because i thought they were wicked.I can remember i didn't want to

I wasn't nice to men, and I didn't care to be. After so many episodes of hurt and pain, I didn't think there was anything left for me to experience. I believed I had already endured the worst.

So, I moved on with my life. Or at least, I thought I did.

But deep inside, I was still hurting—wounded by pain that never seemed to heal. I had convinced myself that I was fine, even when I wasn't.

At twenty years old, I got married and started a family. I thought I knew what I was doing. I believed marriage would finally give me the love and stability I had longed for.

I was wrong.

A Marriage That Felt Like Another Trap

I can't say I was a perfect wife, but I know I did my best. Yet, my best was never enough.

The enemy came after me again—this time through my husband.

Though I was married, I was treated like a prostitute, rejected, and unwanted. It was as if I didn't even exist.

I was married, yet I was completely alone.

I had thought my struggles were over. Instead, they had only just begun.

Depression consumed me once again.

I lost weight, barely eating. My marriage drained the life out of me, leaving me empty. The constant betrayal, rejection, and infidelity broke me in ways I never imagined.

I endured as long as I could, but after years of suffering, I knew I had to leave. If I stayed, depression would destroy me.

Drowning in Alcohol and Sorrow

After leaving my husband, I was still battling depression.

I turned to alcohol, believing it would numb the pain.

At first, it seemed like an escape. But soon, drinking became my best friend—my only comfort.

I had a few friends I hung out with, and every time they saw me, they cheered up because they thought I was fun—the life of the party.

But they had no idea that I was dying inside.

Night after night, I drank my sorrow away, hoping the pain would disappear. But no matter how much I drank, it never did.

I would come home, sit in the darkness, and cry myself to sleep. Then I'd wake up the next day and do it all over again.

For three to four years, I was stuck in this cycle—drowning in my past, unable to break free.

Searching for Healing

During this time, I turned to music.

I started writing, rapping, and singing—pouring my emotions into lyrics. It helped, in some ways. Music became my outlet, a place where I could express what I couldn't say out loud.

But it wasn't enough.

I was still tormented by my past, still suffering from depression. One moment I'd be fine, and the next, I'd drift into deep thoughts, lost in memories that haunted me.

Sadness would hit me out of nowhere, and I couldn't explain it.

I knew I needed help.

I even went to a psychiatrist at one point, but it didn't change anything. I was still broken. I was still depressed.

And then, I tried to take my life again.

That's when I knew something was terribly wrong.

The Answer I Had Been Searching For

No doctor, no therapist, no amount of alcohol could save me.

I needed something greater.

I needed Jesus.

He did for me what no psychiatrist or self-medication could do.

He delivered me from the depression that had consumed my soul.

I prayed.

I cried out to God and told Him I was tired of living this way. I told Him I couldn't do it anymore.

And He answered me.

I opened my heart, and He stepped in.

This version keeps the raw emotion intact while improving readability. Let me know if you'd like me to continue or make any changes!

I wanted nothing to do with men. I saw them as wicked, heartless, and cruel. The thought of interacting with them disgusted me, and when I did, I made sure they felt the same pain I carried inside me.

After so many episodes of hurt and betrayal, I thought I had experienced the worst life had to offer. I believed there was nothing left for me to endure.

I was wrong.

Despite my wounds, I convinced myself that I was fine. I tried to move on, pushing my pain deep inside and pretending it wasn't there. At twenty years old, I got married and started a family. I thought I knew what I was doing. I thought marriage would be a fresh start.

I thought I was finally safe.

But instead of healing, I found myself in another nightmare.

A Marriage That Felt Like a Curse

I can't say I was a perfect wife, but I know I did my best. And yet, my best was never enough.

The enemy came back for me—this time, through my husband.

Even though I was married, I was treated like nothing more than a prostitute. I was rejected, unloved, invisible. It was as if I didn't even exist.

I was married, but I was still alone.

I had believed that my struggles were finally over. But in reality, they had only just begun.

Depression came back stronger than ever.

I lost weight, barely eating. My marriage drained me of life itself. The constant betrayal, the emotional abandonment, the infidelity—I couldn't take it anymore.

After enduring years of a cheating, rejecting husband, I had no choice but to leave. I had to save myself before depression consumed me completely.

Drowning in Alcohol and Pain

But even after leaving, the battle wasn't over.

I was still deeply depressed, and in my desperation, I turned to alcohol.

At first, I thought drinking would help. That maybe, just maybe, it would drown out the pain.

Drinking became my best friend.

I had a few friends I would go out with, and every time they saw me, they cheered up because they thought I was fun—the life of the party.

What they didn't know was that I was dying inside.

Night after night, I would drink my sorrow away, only to come home, sit in the darkness, and cry myself to sleep. Then I would wake up the next day and do it all over again.

For three to four years, I lived like that—stuck in a cycle of pain, drowning in my past, and believing that nothing would ever change.

A Glimmer of Hope

During this time, I started writing music—rapping, singing, putting my emotions into words. It helped, in some ways. Music became an outlet for my pain, a way to release what I couldn't say out loud.

But it wasn't enough.

I was still haunted by my past, still battling depression, still tormented by sadness that would hit me out of nowhere. Some days, I could be happy, and then suddenly, I'd fall into a trance—lost in painful memories, drowning in emotions I couldn't control.

I knew I needed help.

I even saw a psychiatrist at one point, but it didn't make a difference. I was still broken. I was still depressed.

And then, I tried to take my life again.

It was bad.

I knew something was terribly wrong with me.

And in that moment, I realized—no doctor, no therapist, no amount of alcohol could save me.

I needed something greater.

I needed Jesus.

The Answer I Had Been Searching For

Jesus did for me what no psychiatrist, no self-medication, and no coping mechanism ever could.

He delivered me from the depression that had been consuming my soul for years.

I prayed.

I cried out to God and told Him I was tired of living this way. I told Him I couldn't do it anymore.

And He answered me.

I opened my heart, and He stepped in! I wanted to take my pound of Here's a refined version of your passage with improved flow, clarity, and emotional depth:

I saw men as wicked, and I wanted nothing to do with them. When I did interact with them, it was never good—I wasn't kind, and I didn't care to be.

After enduring so much hurt and pain, I believed I had already experienced the worst life had to offer. I thought I had nothing left to go through.

So, I moved on with my life.

Or at least, I thought I did.

But the truth was, I was still deeply wounded. The pain lingered inside me, hidden beneath the surface, but I convinced myself that I was fine.

A Marriage That Brought More Pain

At twenty years old, I got married and started a family. I truly believed I was ready. I thought I knew what I was doing.

I was wrong.

Marriage was supposed to be my fresh start, my safe place, my escape from past pain. Instead, it became another source of heartbreak.

I wasn't perfect, but I know I did my best as a wife. Yet, my best was never enough.

The enemy came after me again—this time through my husband.

Even though I was married, he treated me like I was worthless, as if I was nothing more than an object to be used. The rejection was unbearable.

I was married, yet I felt completely alone.

I had thought my struggles were over. Instead, they had only just begun.

Depression took hold of me again.

I lost weight, barely eating. My marriage drained me, leaving me weak and empty. The betrayal, the constant cheating, the rejection—I couldn't take it anymore.

Eventually, I had no choice but to leave. If I stayed, depression would destroy me.

Drowning in Alcohol and Sorrow

After leaving my husband, I was still battling depression.

I turned to alcohol, thinking it would help numb the pain.

At first, drinking felt like an escape. But soon, it became my best friend—my only comfort.

I had a few friends I hung out with, and every time they saw me, they cheered up because they thought I was funny—the life of the party.

But they had no idea I was dying inside.

Night after night, I drank to forget, hoping the pain would fade. But no matter how much I drank, it never did.

I would come home, sit in the darkness, and cry myself to sleep. Then I'd wake up the next day and do it all over again.

For three to four years, I was stuck in this cycle—drowning in my past, unable to break free.! I drank so much that alcohol became my best friend.

I had a few friends I spent time with, and whenever they saw me, they would cheer up, thinking I was funny and the life of the party. But what they didn't know was that I was battling deep depression.

Night after night, I went out with them, drinking to drown my sorrows—except the pain never went away. No matter how much I drank, it was always there, lingering.

Sometimes, I would come home, sit in the darkness, and cry. Then I would drink even more, hoping the numbness would take over until I drifted off to sleep.

The next day, I would wake up and do it all over again. Here's your passage refined for clarity, flow, and impact while preserving your heartfelt message:

For about three to four years, I lived in depression, drowning in my pain. I turned to music as an outlet—I started writing, rapping, and singing. In some ways, it helped, but not completely. My past still haunted me, and I carried my wounds wherever I went.

I was on a journey, but it wasn't a good one. I still suffered from depression. Some days, I would feel happy, but in the next moment, I would get lost in deep thoughts, slipping into a trance filled with sudden sadness. It was bad. I knew I needed help. But to be honest, the only help I truly needed was Jesus.

I was seeing a psychiatrist at one point, but it didn't seem to help. I was still messed up. I was still depressed. I reached the point where I attempted to take my life again. That's when I knew something was terribly wrong with me. But in the midst of my darkest moment, I found the answer—Jesus. Yes,

Jesus did what no doctor or psychiatrist could do. He delivered me from the chains of depression.

I prayed. I told God I was tired of the way my life was going. And He answered me. I opened up my heart, and I let the Master in. He saved me. And now, I can say with confidence that I do not regret the day I ran to Christ for help—because I was helped, I was set free, I was delivered! Praise the name of Jesus.

So, when you see me, don't envy me. Don't judge me. You don't know the hell I've been through and the battles I've fought just to be here today.

To parents, especially mothers, I have something to say: Please, do not leave your children with just anyone. Pay attention to them. Talk with them. Ask them questions. Know what's happening in their lives. Don't assume they're fine just because they're quiet.

Sometimes, we think we can trust people, but even the Bible warns us not to put our trust in man, but in the Almighty God. And it doesn't matter if you have a son or a daughter—little boys are abused and raped too. Keep your eyes on your children.

The honest truth is, no one can care for your child the way you can. Children can be silent with their parents, but find ways to bond with them so they feel safe enough to confide in you. Don't let them suffer in silence, heading toward suicide or depression. This is serious. The fight is real. The enemy is real. And depression is Here's your passage refined for clarity, structure, and impact while preserving your heartfelt message:

Depression is real. And not everyone is able to recognize it or come out of it. Some don't make it out alive because depression can lead to suicide, and suicide leads to death. That's why it's better to know what's going on with your child and offer them help—whether it's counseling, psychiatric support, or leading them to Jesus. I can't tell you how to help your own child, but I can say this: if you try Jesus, He won't fail you.

Whatever you do, don't leave them alone in their struggles. Find out what's going on in their lives. It's your duty as a parent to know—unless you're in a situation where you truly can't. And if you can't, then be bold enough to ask for help from someone who can care for them. Show them the love they need and deserve, because children don't just want love—they need it.

If they don't get it from you, they will seek it elsewhere. Whether from an aunt, a friend, or even a stranger, they will look for love. And that's how so many end up in dangerous situations, being used and abused. Many women suffer daily in abusive relationships, and even men go through this—simply because they were searching for love in the wrong places.

Look at the young girls who turn to prostitution. Why? Because they want to feel needed, to be loved. They crave the attention their parents didn't give them. And before they realize it, they're trapped. Many of them never intended to end up on a stripper pole or selling their bodies—it started with a desire for love and acceptance.

The same is true for many drug dealers. If you look deeper, you'll find that most of them didn't grow up with stable parents to guide them. They felt rejected, so they turned to the streets, to drugs, to crime—searching for love, attention, and satisfaction. We assume they're just in it for the money, but many of them aren't. They're looking for something more, something they can't even define. But deep down, it's love they're after.

Have you ever wondered why love is the greatest commandment in the Bible? It's because love is the most powerful force—it covers a multitude of sins, it heals wounds, and it conquers all.

The pain we feel as children doesn't just disappear when we become adults. It lingers. It shapes us. And if it's not dealt with early, it becomes a stumbling block in life. Some people don't want to admit that the pain they're carrying started in childhood—maybe because it's embarrassing. But whether we admit it or not, it's there. And if left untreated, it doesn't just vanish. It grows into something worse.

It can manifest as depression, bipolar disorder, or even schizophrenia. Pain, if left unhealed, spreads like a disease. Think about it—when an illness isn't treated in time, it worsens. Some tumors are benign, but others are malignant and spread to vital organs. Pain and trauma work the same way.

If we don't deal with them, they metastasize, affecting not just our lives but the lives of those around us.

Hurt people hurt people. If they don't find healing, they often pass their pain onto others. But here's the good news—pain doesn't have to be a permanent part of your life. Healing is possible. Some wounds can't be healed by doctors, but they can be healed by God's divine power.

That's why we must work on ourselves before trying to help others. If we don't, we risk making things worse. The Bible says, "Remove the plank from your own eye before trying to remove the speck from your brother's." While we're busy pointing fingers at others, we often fail to realize that we're just as broken.

May 8th—My Birthday

It's Wednesday, May 8th—my birthday. But to be honest, it doesn't feel like a happy day. With so much on my mind, I barely slept the night before. Even after waking up, I still felt like I needed more sleep. So, with no real plans for my birthday, I went back to bed.

I had a few admirers and some empty promises, but nothing certain. I didn't expect much from the day—not with everything going on in my life. Then, unexpectedly, my phone rang. It was my birthday date.

I was surprised. I didn't think I had one.

He had someone in mind to take me out for the day, and I agreed. I wasn't really excited—not because I didn't want to celebrate, but because it felt like my world was upside down. Still, I decided to get ready.

I searched for something appropriate to wear, got my hair done, took a bath, and later in the day, I got a few more calls—but not many. It wasn't long before my date arrived to pick me up.

He stepped out of the car, wished me a happy birthday, gave me a hug, and opened the door for me.

This version maintains your raw emotion and powerful message but improves readability, structure, and impact. Let me know if you'd like any changes! I Here's a more polished and structured version of your passage with improved grammar, clarity, and flow:

As we sat down, we drove off, but funny enough, it wasn't planned—we didn't really know where to go. He wasn't from the area, and I wasn't in the mood to do anything fancy. I just wanted to get out of the house, to clear my mind from everything that was going on.

He kindly asked me where I wanted to go, and I said Wendy's. It was one of my favorite fast-food spots. I really liked Red Lobster too, but in the mood I was in, I just wanted something simple. More than anything, I just needed to get out of that house.

So, I got my favorite meal from Wendy's, sat in the car, and ate with the windows down and the roof open. The car was parked facing the beauty of nature—trees, plants, and the fresh, open air. It was a beautiful sight. After eating, we sat and chatted for a while before driving down to the beach.

At the beach, we parked, sat in the car for a bit, then got out and walked around. After a while, we returned to the car, talked some more, and just took in the peaceful view of the ocean. I let the calmness of nature soothe me for as long as I could.

Eventually, we left and went to a buffet. The food was delicious, but even as I ate, I could still feel the pain in my heart. The situation I was going through was screaming at me, making it hard to enjoy the moment.

After dinner, we decided to relax some more outside a Wawa store, chatting and making a few phone calls. But as it got closer to the time for me to go home, I could feel the pain, hurt, and discomfort settling in my stomach. I didn't want to go back. I wished the day wouldn't end, but unfortunately, it was coming to a close.

When we arrived at the house, he walked me in. He saw the look of sadness, hurt, and pain on my face. He encouraged me to stay strong, as I always tried to do. I couldn't hold back my tears—I cried and thanked him for his words of encouragement before slowly walking upstairs.

As soon as I stepped inside, I could hear noises from downstairs. A strange feeling came over me—an overwhelming sense that I wasn't welcome. I was living with my elder sister and her husband at the time, but suddenly, I felt like an enemy in the house.

I ignored the signs, pretending I didn't see or feel what was happening, even though my gut was wrenching with unease. I kept asking myself, What in the world is going on? All of a sudden, I was being treated like an outcast.

But the Word of God says, We wrestle not against flesh and blood, but against principalities, against powers, against the rulers of the darkness of this world, and against spiritual wickedness in high places. So, I decided not to respond. Instead, I stayed calm, prayed that God would save me, and acted as if I didn't notice what was happening.

At that point, my sister and her husband had stopped talking to me altogether. Whenever they saw me, they would start screaming and speaking in tongues, claiming they were fighting off a witch that was attacking them. I guess, in their eyes, I was that witch.

Still, I played it safe and ignored them.

Later that night, I decided to change into my nightgown for bed when my sister's husband approached me.

"Don't close the door," he said. "No more locking the door."

I calmly responded, "How am I supposed to change my clothes then? You mean I should change with the door open while everyone can see me? I have no privacy."

"Yes," he replied. "Leave the door open. Don't close it."

I was stunned. No more privacy? This was crazy. I knew then, without a doubt, that things were out of control. But I still decided to do what made sense—I closed the door to change, planning to open it again once I was done.

But as soon as I started changing—BAM! There was a loud knock, and before I could react, the door swung wide open. He had pushed it open without a care, despite the fact that I was half-dressed.

"I said don't close the door!" he yelled.

At first, I didn't understand what was happening. But after everything I witnessed that night, it became clearer and clearer—I was being treated like a witch.

I was about to lie down when I suddenly heard someone running up the stairs. It was my sister's husband, and moments later, she joined him. They were both speaking in tongues—or so they claimed—before he suddenly lashed out angrily, like a hungry lion ready to tear me apart.

"GET OUT! GET OUT! You have to get out! You have until Saturday to leave my house!" he shouted.

Surprisingly, I remained calm. I simply said, "Okay," and started packing my things. Even though I had no idea where I was going to go and it was freezing outside, I knew I had no choice.

I texted my friend Tony to let him know what was happening.

"The time has finally come," I wrote.

He responded, "For what?"

"Remember what I told you a month ago? That I felt like they wanted to kick me out? Well, my spirit was right. It's happening now."

He texted back in shock. "What do you mean?"

"You heard me right. My sister's husband told me to leave on my birthday. He said I have until Saturday."

"Wow! I can't believe what you're saying," he replied.

"Well, believe it," I responded.

Then he asked, "How long will it take you to—"leave

Tony asked, "How long will it take you to pack your stuff?"

I replied, "Not too long."

He said, "I'm coming back for you. Get your stuff ready."

I said, "Okay," and I began packing.

In my mind, I thought I had packed everything, but in reality, almost half of my belongings were still there. I was too confused to remember everything. So much was going on in my mind at once that I couldn't possibly focus on packing properly. I truly believed I had grabbed all my things because I didn't want to have to return to that place—a place where I was no longer welcome.

The drive that night felt long, and my mind was racing. What just happened? Where am I going? What will become of me? The uncertainty weighed heavily on me.

Then, in the midst of my anxious thoughts, I heard a calm, still voice say, "Let not your heart be troubled."

I knew it was my Father speaking to me. At that moment, I felt a sense of relief—I wasn't alone, even though I felt so alone.

It was around 3 a.m. when we arrived in New York at the house I knew I would return to someday, though I never thought it would be this soon. Mentally, I was overwhelmed, but I held on to my faith in God. He had never failed me before, and I knew He wouldn't fail me now—not when I needed Him the most.

And He didn't fail me.

He came through for me, as He always does.

There are days when I wonder, What's next? And there are days when I remind myself of His promises, casting my cares aside. The situation wasn't comfortable, but I kept declaring:

"The best is yet to come! This too shall pass! This is not permanent! My story will someday be a thing of the past! Victory is mine!"

Still, there were moments when I had to cry out, "Lord, give me more of Your strength."

No situation is permanent—especially when you exercise patience and fight your battles on your knees. When you're going through hardship, it can feel like your breakthrough will never come, like the pain will never end. But believe me when I say—that's when you have to put your trust in God, stand firm in His promises, and let praise bring you through to your moment of victory.

Think about Joseph—thrown into a pit and then sold into slavery. He didn't know what to expect or what his future held, but he never gave up. He didn't focus on his situation; instead, he made the best of it while trusting in God. He was too busy being used by God to complain.

That's the kind of faith I strive for.

When you can shift your focus from your pain to your purpose, that's when you know you won't be defeated. You were born to win and destined for greatness.

Everyone can fight, but not everyone is a winner.

And not every battle is the same.

At some point in life, you will have to fight—just as I did, just as David did. You can't afford to lose. The more you fight, the stronger you become—not because you're fighting in your own strength, but because the Spirit of God is fighting for you. Victory is certain. But you have to bring out the warrior in you.

There's a time for everything. A time to be silent and a time to speak. A time to endure and a time to fight back. You have to discern the season you're in so you know how to handle it.

So how do you know when it's time to fight?

It's when the same problem keeps staring you in the face, refusing to leave until you do something about it.

And how do you fight back?

Matthew 17:20—Jesus said, "Because you have so little faith. Truly I tell you, if you have faith as small as a mustard seed, you can say to this mountain, 'Move from here to there,' and it will move. Nothing will be impossible for you."

With faith and the Word of God, you can command your problems to leave—and they will obey.

Growing up, I didn't know much about faith or spiritual warfare. But as you mature, you begin to understand what life is truly about—what makes sense and what doesn't. That's why babies eat baby food, while adults eat solid food.

1 Corinthians 13:11 says, "When I was a child, I spoke as a child; but when I became a man, I put away childish things."

As far back as I can remember, I was a quiet child. I never spoke up, even when I was treated unfairly. I never defended myself. But if I got into a fight, I would fight. That fighter spirit was always in me, even though, at some point, I lost my voice.

I had to learn how to get my voice back.

What do I mean by that?

As a child, I couldn't express my feelings—even when I wanted to. Speaking up could easily get you punished. It was as if children weren't even allowed to have an opinion.

I remember one time when my mom was complaining to me about my brother's wife. As she spoke, I realized she was wrong in the situation. So I told her, "Mom, you were wrong for doing that."

She immediately screamed at me. "Shut up! What do you know about right or wrong?"

She wanted to beat me just for telling her the truth. I ran.

That moment taught me something.

As a child, I had no voice. I had to stay quiet—even when I saw injustice.

But as an adult, things changed. Now, I fight for justice.

As a child in school, I was picked on and mocked. The kids from my community would tease me, calling me "Miss Pearl Donkey." I hated it. They would lie about me to my mother just to get me in trouble. And the worst part? She would believe them. I got punished for things I never did.

That experience also taught me something: people will lie on you for no reason.

But there is a reason.

When you're anointed from your mother's womb, when you're destined for greatness, people will pick on you, lie about you, and try to break you. I went through all of that.

They called me Miss Pearl Donkey because I did a lot of hard labor—carrying heavy loads to and from the farm, burdens that even a donkey would struggle with. I don't know how I carried them, but I did. If I didn't, I would be punished.

Looking back now, I see that it was God who gave me the strength.

Even through those hard times, He was there.

When I cried—He was there.

When I felt lost—He was there.

When I thought I couldn't go any further—He was there.

When I felt suicidal—He was there.

And that's why I made it this far. Because He was right there.

Even when life gets tough, God will walk with you through the storm. He will carry you through the pressure.

The weight of it all was on me.

But God was right there.

Here's a more structured and polished version of your passage. I've corrected grammar errors, improved clarity, and made it more engaging while keeping your voice and message intact.

Sometimes, when I look back on everything I've been through, I ask myself, How did I make it? But the answer is always the same—Yah was right there with me.

There were days when I dreaded going home from school because home wasn't a place of peace or joy for me. It felt like a place of constant depression. If I came home even a minute past the expected time, I'd get beaten. At one point, it felt like no matter what I did, I was always in the wrong. I would get punished whether I deserved it or not. It got to a point where I felt immune to the punishment—it became an expectation rather than a consequence.

That experience shaped me. I no longer allow people to mistreat me, lie on me, or beat me down for no reason. A fighter was born in me. I developed the spirit of a warrior. Now, I am not afraid to stand up for the truth. I have learned that many people don't like correction. They resist rebuke and sometimes even hate the one who brings the truth. But I will stand for truth, whether it is welcomed or not.

Hebrews 12:6 says, "For the Lord disciplines the one He loves, and He chastens everyone He accepts as His son." One of the ways He chastens us is by speaking truth—whether through His word or through someone else. Yet, I've realized that if the spirit of truth is not in you, it can be difficult to either tell the truth or accept it.

In life, always stand for truth and righteousness. When you do, you reflect the character of Jesus, the Father of Truth. When you choose lies and deception, you align yourself with Satan, the father of lies. Standing for truth isn't always easy, but in the end, it is worth it.

I firmly believe that what you practice, you become. What you feed your spirit, you reflect in your life. Every trial, tribulation, and temptation we endure serves a purpose—it teaches us resilience and determination. There is a fighter birthed from pain. After all, if there were no war, there would be no need for weapons.

Difficult experiences teach us lessons we would never have learned otherwise. Life has knocked me down many times, but by God's grace, I have always gotten back up. The speed at which we rise may differ—we may get up quickly, or we may take time to heal—but the important thing is that we rise.

Falling down gives us a unique perspective. It allows us to see life from a different angle. And as we rise, we encounter new challenges, but those struggles shape us. Our experiences, both good and bad, mold us into who we are meant to be.

I have spent years in uncomfortable situations—not by choice, but by life's journey. I have worked jobs I didn't like, but even in those places, I learned valuable lessons. One of the toughest jobs I ever had was working as a housekeeper in a hotel. Until I did it myself, I never realized how difficult that job truly was.

Some days, I would come in to find 18 to 20 rooms assigned to me, all of which had to be cleaned by 4 PM. Most mornings, I skipped breakfast, surviving only on a cup of coffee. I worked through the day without a lunch break, determined to finish on time. By the time I got home—sometimes as late as 10 or 11 PM after overtime—I was too exhausted to eat dinner. I would fall asleep in my work clothes, only to wake up at 5:30 AM to do it all over again.

Even on my days off, they would call me in because they were short-staffed. And as if the workload wasn't hard enough, I also had to deal with supervisors constantly hovering over me, ensuring my work met their standards.

One day, I was cleaning a room when I stumbled upon blood-soaked sheets and towels. There was so much blood that it was terrifying. I had to call my housekeeping manager immediately. It was moments like that that made me question if I could keep going.

But through it all, I learned something valuable—sometimes, we find ourselves in places we don't want to be, but every experience teaches us something. After working in that job, I never looked at housekeepers the same way again. Whenever I stay in a hotel now, I make an effort not to leave the room messy out of respect for the people who will have to clean it.

I also learned humility. I know what it feels like to be overlooked, to have people walk past you as if you are invisible, as if you are less than they are. But I have come to realize that no one is less than anyone else.

Life will put you through tough situations, but those situations don't define you. How you respond to them does. I've been through storms, and I've felt broken.

But every time I thought I couldn't make it, God was right there, carrying me through. And that's why I'm still standing today. Here's a refined version of your passage while keeping your voice, message, and emotions intact:

After leaving my previous job for many reasons, I picked up another one at a beauty supply store. It was part-time, so I decided to work there while searching for something else. Finding a job wasn't easy, especially with my situation—expired documents made it even more challenging. But I held on to the one I had because the timing was perfect. It didn't take me away from God's presence, church, or prayer.

At first glance, the job seemed simple and harmless, but I soon realized I had walked into a spiritual battlefield. It was like stepping into a den of lions without knowing. Everything looked normal on the outside, but in the spirit, it was an entirely different story. Every day at work felt like a battle. It was warfare. And strangely, it seemed like I was the only one who could see it. No one else had a clue about what was happening in the spirit.

The moment I stepped foot into the shop, the attacks began. I saw different spirits manifesting through people. They looked like regular humans, but I could discern something else operating behind them—unfamiliar, dark spirits. They viewed me as a disturbance, but at first, I didn't understand why. So I prayed. And then the answer came.

It wasn't anything I did that disturbed them. It was simply my presence—my essence—my prayers. The fact that I prayed in their city, in that very store, troubled them. In the spirit, they saw me as a troublemaker. They even held meetings about me, plotting how they could get rid of me. But their plans failed.

They tried to scare me away, but it didn't work. I am not a coward.

They tried manifesting who they really were, but that didn't work either.

They even tried to physically knock me out at work, but still, it didn't work.

Each time they failed, they sent someone new. But no matter who they sent, they could not touch me. Why? Because I was protected by the Most High,

Yahweh. He had already declared that they could not touch me, and His word stands forever.

These were not just ordinary people. They came in the flesh, but they carried spiritual powers and ranks in the kingdom of darkness. It wasn't an easy experience, and it took the grace of God and the power of the Holy Spirit to stand firm without fear. But instead of being fearful, I was more prayerful.

Because I know greater is He that is in me than he that is in the world (1 John 4:4).

I later realized they were part of an occult group, and their mission was simple: destroy God's servant. But how can they destroy what they did not create? They always believe they have more power than God, but they are deceived. Can I blame them? No. Because they serve the father of lies.

Satan has convinced his followers that he is greater than God. But if they truly understood the Word, they would see that even Satan himself acknowledges that he is not the Most High—he only wants to be like Him.

In Isaiah 14:14, Satan said, "I will ascend above the heights of the clouds; I will be like the Most High."

Did you catch that? "I will be like the Most High."

That means even he knows he is not the Most High!

His goal has always been to deceive. Isaiah 14:12 says, "How art thou fallen from heaven, O Lucifer, son of the morning! How art thou cut down to the ground, which didst weaken the nations!"

Satan's assignment is to weaken the nations, to kill, steal, and destroy (John 10:10). He works hard to prove that he has power, but he can only go as far as God allows. He still needs permission from God to do certain things.

In the book of Job (Job 1:6-12), Satan had to ask God for permission to attack Job. He admitted that God had placed a hedge of protection around Job that he could not penetrate. That alone proves who is in control.

And that's why Satan and his followers try to convince people that the Bible isn't real. They don't want people to know the truth about Yahweh and His power.

It's just like an employee who works for a billionaire boss. Imagine that one day, the employee starts lying, pretending to be the boss. If no one actually knows the real boss personally, they might believe the lie.

That's exactly what Satan does.

But I give God all the glory because I know who the real Boss is.

What I Did:

- Fixed grammatical and punctuation errors for smoother reading.
- Clarified ideas to make them more impactful.
- Enhanced readability by breaking long sentences into shorter, more engaging ones.
- Maintained your voice and emotions while making the story flow better.

This version keeps your testimony powerful, clear, and compelling. Let me know if you'd like any adjustments! Here's a more structured and grammatically polished version of your passage while keeping your voice and message intact:

Many lies have been told, but I'm thankful that I know Jesus is the way, the truth, and the life (John 14:6). Even though this truth is clearly stated in Scripture, some people still believe there are many ways to God. But how can they believe otherwise if they are listening to the father of lies? My prayer is that one day, those people will have an encounter with God—just as even Satan himself had an encounter with Him and was able to ask the questions he wanted.

This experience at my job allowed me to grow and learn many things I didn't know before. It wasn't my favorite job, but I was placed there for a reason, and when my time was up and my assignment was over, I left in victory once again, in Jesus' name. I wasn't fired—I left peacefully, as God directed me. By the time I was leaving, my boss had become a different person. He had found peace in Christ. Salvation had come to him. From playing secular music in his store, he switched to gospel music. What a mighty God we serve!

One thing I've noticed more and more is that when you allow God to use you and let His light shine through you, it radiates—even through the thickest darkness. It shines so brightly that it affects those around you. You don't even have to do much—just be willing for God to use you for His glory.

After leaving this job, I was sure Satan was upset with me. He went and planned another attack because he hates what God is using me to do in people's lives. But I fear no evil because God is with me. I reached another level in God, and with that came new battles.

Shortly after leaving my job, I focused solely on Yah's work. But then I faced another challenge—I was kicked out of my apartment. My sister had gotten into a dispute with my landlord's aunt, and because of the tension, my landlord asked me to leave. At the time, I had nowhere else to go.

I went through what felt like hell on earth. I ended up staying with a friend of my sister and his kids. Oh boy, it was not easy. I went from having my own bed to sleeping on a couch—not even a room to myself. I was basically living in their living room, and it was a real struggle. Many times, I was locked out when I left the house. Sometimes, I wouldn't even be able to get in at all and had to find somewhere else to sleep for the night.

Eventually, I was able to get an apartment, but since I wasn't working at the time, I couldn't afford furniture—not even a bed. I ended up sleeping on the floor. I started thinking about how I would buy some furniture because I had no financial help. That's when I decided to do food delivery. It was a job where you worked on your own, but there was a major challenge—I didn't have a car, a bike, or even a scooter.

So, I decided I would walk.

Yes, I said it—I walked to deliver people's Postmates food orders.

If I had a car, each delivery would have taken around five minutes. But because I was walking, it took me 20 to 30 minutes just to drop off one order. Then, I'd have to walk all the way back to the food court to get the next order. Because deliveries took so long, the most I could complete in a day was six—not even ten. Each delivery paid between four and six dollars, and with a tip, I could sometimes get up to ten dollars.

It wasn't much.

To make things worse, I didn't have a power bank, so when my phone battery got too low, I had to stop working and go home.

Now that is what you call hard work—extremely hard work.

And still, the money wasn't enough to pay my rent.

Eventually, I got kicked out again.

For a period of time, I was homeless.

I moved from one park to another, trying to pass the time because I had nowhere to go. Sometimes, I would go to Wendy's and sit there all day just to have a place to stay. Here's a refined and well-structured version of your passage while keeping your voice and message intact:

When night fell, I would walk to a park and sit there until morning. At sunrise, I would find a friend's house to shower before hitting the road again. I can truly say I know what it's like to be homeless, and it was no joke—especially since it wasn't summer, but winter. So, when I caught pneumonia, I wasn't surprised. I knew exactly why.

I remember one particular day in the park. I was sitting there as usual when, out of nowhere, the rain came pouring down heavily. As it drenched me, I broke down in tears, crying out to God. It was an unforgettable, jaw-dropping experience.

When my sister kicked me out and blocked me, she thought she was doing me harm. But what she didn't realize was that she was pushing me into my rising season—my season of learning and breakthrough. After she kicked me out, I enrolled in school, completed my program, and earned my certificate. In that same season, I obtained four different certificates of completion. My breakthrough was right around the corner.

And thank God for His grace—I didn't give up.

One night, while I was home, minding my own business and browsing my phone, God was minding my business too—but in a different way. A message came in via WhatsApp from a man of God. He told me that I was among the list of people chosen by God as candidates for ordination.

I was overwhelmed with joy!

To know that God saw me fit to carry His word—it is the greatest honor a person can receive. It wasn't man who chose me, but God Himself. Where men may see you as unqualified, God sees you as qualified—not based on money, status, or connections, but by His divine will. That's why I always say: He qualifies the called.

If it were up to man, it would never be so. But thank God, it's not a man's pick—it's a God's hand-pick!

After everything I had been through, after never giving up, I lived to see the day that God honored me. Wow!

There were so many battles before this moment. The process was not easy, but thank God—I passed the test of time. I faced trials, temptations, persecutions, and intense spiritual battles. But Jesus is the winner man, all the time!

I remember one battle in particular. I came face to face with a witch who was trying to take what rightfully belonged to me—my womb. She attempted a spiritual exchange, trying to steal the children God had promised me. Maybe she didn't know who I was, or maybe witches have become so bold and upfront with their wickedness.

But I was on high alert. I knew what was happening.

I always say, keep your Holy Ghost gun ready to fire because the kingdom of God suffers violence, and the violent take it by force (Matthew 11:12). I had to fight like David in this battle—every single day, contending for the destiny of my unborn children.

This witch tried everything to take them spiritually. But I fought back.

Until one day, I heard her say, "What kind of power is she using? Her power is so strong—I want that kind of power."

That day, she realized she had lost the battle. She probably thought I was doing the same evil she was doing, but no—this power is Holy Ghost power! Glory be to God!

So if you've been going through some battles, don't give up. It's taking you somewhere. It's taking you to your victory.

Always remember: If everything in your life seems too good, too calm, too quiet—something might be off. But if all hell is breaking loose around you, if battles are coming from every direction—that means you're doing something that pleases God. Keep going!

One thing you should know: The devil does not fight you if he already has you.

He doesn't attack people who aren't doing anything for God. He fights when you're walking in obedience, when you're aligned with God's will. And his number one strategy is distraction. He wants to shift your focus from God's work to the chaos he's stirring in your life.

He will use anything—your mom, your sister, your friend, your husband, your job, even your boss at work. As long as it can be used as a distraction, he'll use it. So be careful for nothing (Philippians 4:6) and remain prayerful, so you're never caught off guard.

No matter what happens in your life, always be thankful and prayerful.

God is the ultimate. When the enemy tries to confuse and bombard us with obstacles, always remember—God is the obstacle remover. He will clear every stumbling block so we can soar like the eagles we were meant to be.

I can tell you this from experience.

The enemy starts early, trying to steal from us what rightfully belongs to us.

Let me share a story.

I was only fourteen years old when I decided that I was not going back home. I was tired of being treated unfairly. I felt helpless, so I made up my mind—I was not going back.

That night, when I didn't return, it was a big alarm. The police got involved. But I was hiding at my cousin's house. After some time, I felt sorry for the woman my mom had left me with. I knew she wouldn't know what to tell my mom when she called and found out I was missing. So, I called and told her, "I'm safe, but I'm not coming back."

She had no choice but to relay the message.

Of course, after I ran away, everyone suddenly wanted to know why. Now they were paying attention.

I thought to myself: When I was being treated like a slave every day, no one intervened. But the moment I ran away, I got everyone's attention.

Now they were begging me to come back. But why?

Because they weren't the ones being treated like a slave—I was.

They didn't care about how I felt. They only cared about their mother having someone to take care of her. It was never about me.

So that's why I left.

I continued my education where I was, and for the first time, I felt a sense of freedom.

Later, when I went back to visit, she was furious. It was as if she was saying, How dare you leave? Who will be my slave now that you're gone?

It was heartbreaking. I never knew people could be so wicked.

But welcome to life.

To take revenge, she decided she would burn my American passport. Yes—you heard me right. She said she was going to burn it.

But God sent an angel to save it!

When she went to destroy it, she couldn't find it. God had hidden it from her.

Years later, when I was ready to travel again, I went to retrieve it from the very person God had used to protect it.

And that's how I was able to travel. Your story is incredibly powerful, and the way you've overcome so many obstacles is inspiring. Below is a revised version of your text with better structure, grammar, and flow while keeping your voice and testimony intact.

After that, I traveled to the U.S., and let me tell you—it was a crazy experience. That wasn't the only thing my adoptive mother tried to destroy. She held onto my documents, and without them, I couldn't get into school. This delay kept me from finishing my education in Jamaica, and people used to wonder why I wasn't in school. The truth is, I didn't have the necessary documents to enroll.

That's how the enemy works—using people to delay and destroy you from an early age. It wasn't just a normal situation; there was a spirit behind all that wickedness. Evil forces were trying to break me down physically, spiritually, emotionally, and mentally. That's why, as a young girl, I constantly battled suicidal thoughts. The enemy wanted me dead and buried—but God!

After traveling to America, I experienced even more setbacks and delays. I felt like I was in a spiritual prison for years. God had poured so many ideas into me, but every time I tried to move forward, I hit a dead end. I would start something, and just when I thought it was taking off, everything would crash—like a car wreck. And it wasn't normal.

I met important people along the way, but they never saw me for who I truly was. It was as if I was invisible. Most of them walked away thinking I had no ambition, no vision. Imagine carrying so much inside of you—dreams, gifts, and potential—but no one sees it. That was my battle. Alongside that, I faced deep rejection, which only made things worse.

For years, I felt stuck and stagnant. It was as if something was holding me down every time I tried to rise. But believe me when I say, I prayed and took action. Because faith without works is dead. I fought my battles on my knees, and God gave me the victory. The enemy wanted me in one place—silent, without using my gifts. But I refused. I declared, "Not so, devil! You belong under my feet."

So I fought. I fasted. I prayed. And I sought the Lord for His guidance. And guess what? He answered. He gave me instructions, and when I obeyed, I received my breakthrough.

For a long time, I felt trapped in America. At one point, I even asked God, "Is this really Your plan for me?" Deep down, I knew it wasn't. Then, finally, the day came when I was able to travel again. I almost couldn't believe it! God had broken the gates of iron and brass, and I was free to fly.

When I arrived at the airport, I was still in disbelief. But when I boarded that plane without any problems, I knew—this was victory. I didn't even care where I was flying to; I just wanted to be free. And freedom is exactly what I felt.

That trip was the beginning of something new. From not traveling at all for ten years, I went from country to country. It was surreal. At one point, I thought, "Wow, am I dreaming?" But no—it was my reality. Sometimes you can be stuck in one place for so long, feeling stagnant, and then suddenly, God moves you in ways you never expected. One moment, you feel trapped, and the next, you're traveling so much that you're asking God to slow it down.

This was a new life for me—a life of faith. And I would call it faith on the edge because I left with no job, no home, and no family waiting for me. It was just me, my faith, and God. The Bible says that faith is the substance of things hoped for, the evidence of things not seen (Hebrews 11:1). And let me tell you—if you can see how everything is going to work out, then it's not faith.

I learned firsthand that you have to be careful what you pray for. If you ask God to teach you how to trust Him, you better be ready—because you don't know how He will answer that prayer. He might take you on a journey where you have no choice but to trust Him completely.

There were times when I had no one to call. And even when I tried, there was no answer. But every time I said, "Father," He answered, "Here I am."

God positioned me in situations where I had no choice but to depend on Him. No job, no steady income—just faith. And yet, He provided. I had food to eat, clothes to wear, and a place to lay my head.

This revision makes your testimony clearer and more engaging while keeping your powerful storytelling intact. Let me know if you'd like me to tweak anything further! Your experiences are intense, eye-opening, and full of powerful lessons. Below is a revised version of your story, improving the structure, grammar, and clarity while maintaining your voice and emotions.

By the grace of my Father, God, everything I needed was provided—even someone to drive me around whenever I needed to go somewhere. My first stop was Nigeria, a country that had been on my list for a long time. I was excited to finally visit, but what I experienced was unlike anything I had ever seen before.

From the moment I landed, it felt like I had stepped into Daniel in the lions' den. The confusion started right at the airport. Even though I had taken my COVID-19 test before traveling, they insisted I pay for another one upon arrival. I was shocked. "What is going on?" I thought. Someone standing nearby turned to me and said, "Welcome to Nigeria."

After going through immigration, customs, and all the necessary protocols, I finally made it to baggage claim—only to be met with relentless begging. I gave what I had, thinking that would be enough, but the begging continued outside. They had no shame about it. It was overwhelming. I had just come off a long flight, exhausted, hungry, and needing rest, yet they wouldn't even let me breathe.

When I finally arrived at my lodging, I was relieved. I could shower, eat, and rest—thank God.

My Experience in Nigeria

Wanting to explore, I took a cab to see what Nigeria was all about. I saw beautiful places, but I also saw so much suffering. Many people were just trying to survive, hustling day to day. I saw young children begging on the streets under the hot sun while their parents sat in the shade. What broke my heart even more was that they truly believed this was their destiny—to beg.

Most of these families were Muslim, and while not all Muslims or Nigerians lived this way, it was mostly Muslims I saw in this condition. Nigeria is a country of extremes. You have those who are extremely wealthy and get whatever they want, and then you have those who endure hardship daily—from the police to the system itself. Corruption is rampant, and it needs to stop.

After witnessing the suffering around me, I decided it was time to leave. But leaving Nigeria was not as easy as I thought.

The Battle to Leave Nigeria

When I arrived at the airport for my flight, I was told I couldn't board. "But why?" I asked. Their excuses made no sense. It was clear they were just looking for ways to extort money from me.

Frustrated, I left, got everything they asked for, and returned for my second attempt at leaving. Again, they denied me. By this time, I had already extended my stay twice, and I needed to go.

On my third attempt, things got even worse.

On the way to the airport, the police pulled over my taxi, claiming the driver had made a wrong turn. Instead of giving him a ticket, they ordered him to move to the passenger seat while they took over the driver's seat! I sat in the back, watching everything unfold in disbelief. They demanded money from him, and when he said he didn't have it, they refused to let him go.

I was running out of time. My flight was leaving soon, and here I was, stuck on the roadside because of police corruption. I prayed, "God, release Your fire upon this police officer. Make him let us go!"

A minute later, he received a call from his colleagues and had to leave. That was how we finally got back on the road.

When I arrived at the airport, the battle continued. They wanted me to pay more money just to get on my own flight. They claimed my COVID-19 test was invalid, just so I would be forced to buy another one from them.

I could feel the spiritual warfare all around me. The principalities were real. The darkness was thick. Right there in the airport, I did what I do best—I called on the name of Jesus.

And He delivered me.

After endless delays, corruption, and obstacles, I finally made it onto my flight. Sitting in my seat, I silently rejoiced. I praised God for fighting that battle for me. I told myself, "I will never return to Nigeria unless it is God's will." I had seen firsthand how hard Nigerians had to fight just to live, just to survive. That day, I gained a deeper understanding of the spiritual battles in that country. Only God can truly deliver someone from that kind of oppression.

Arrival in South Africa

After Nigeria, my next stop was South Africa, a country I had always dreamed of visiting. I specifically wanted to see Cape Town.

The moment I arrived, I could feel the difference. Everything was smooth—from immigration to customs to baggage claim. No one was harassing me. No one was begging me for money. I thought to myself, Wow, what a huge difference between these two countries.

Driving through the city, I was in awe of God's creation—the mountains, the trees, the fresh breeze. The peace I felt was unmatched. I checked into a hotel in the city center, where I had easy access to food and everything I needed. But the best part? My hotel room had a breathtaking view of Table Mountain.

Each morning, I woke up to the sight of that majestic mountain. As the sun rose and shone upon it, I could feel God's presence. When the clouds sat perfectly on the mountaintop at noon, it was a reminder of His glory. Every time I looked up, I couldn't help but praise His name.

One of my small goals was to climb Table Mountain. When the opportunity finally came, I was overjoyed. Standing at the top, looking down at the world below, I felt such a deep connection to God.

I took a few pictures, and in one of them, I noticed something supernatural—a rainbow over me. It was as if God Himself was saying, "Hello, Simone. I remember My promise to you."

The Beauty of God's Creation

After experiencing the mountain, I visited the beach, surrounded by God's creation—rocks, trees, and the endless ocean. It was healing.

In that moment, I reflected on everything I had been through—from the battles in Nigeria to the peace in South Africa. One country showed me the depth of human struggle, while the other reminded me of God's tranquility and provision.

Through it all, I had learned a powerful lesson: No matter where you go, God is with you. He fights for you. He provides for you. And He will always make a way.! Awesome! Here's a rewritten section using the structured approach:

A Journey of Faith Across Nations

Divine Provision and Stepping Out in Faith

From the moment I set out on this journey, I knew I had to trust God completely. I had no steady income, no fixed plans, and no guarantees—only faith. Yet, my Father in heaven provided everything I needed. If I needed a ride, someone appeared to take me where I needed to go. If I needed food, He sent provision. Every need was met, reminding me daily that I was living a life of faith, just like the disciples when Jesus sent them out with nothing but trust in God's provision.

Nigeria: A Test of Faith and Spiritual Warfare

Nigeria had always been on my list of places to visit, and when I finally arrived, I was excited. But from the moment I stepped off the plane, I realized this was going to be an experience like no other. It was as if I had walked into the den of lions, just like Daniel.

At the airport, the confusion started. Despite having already taken a required COVID-19 test before arrival, I was asked to pay for another one. Shocked,

I questioned what was going on. A voice from nearby said, "Welcome to Nigeria." It was my first taste of what was to come.

As I went through immigration and customs, I faced continuous requests for money. Even outside the airport, people shamelessly begged without restraint. I was exhausted from my flight, hungry, and in need of rest, yet I was being harassed for money at every turn. It was overwhelming.

Despite the frustration, I settled into my lodging and prepared to explore Nigeria. I saw both the beauty and the struggles of the country. There were stunning places, but there was also deep suffering. I saw young children begging in the hot sun while their parents sat in the shade, watching them. Many of these families were Muslim, and they believed begging was their destiny. My heart broke for them.

The divide in Nigeria was extreme—there were the very rich who had everything, and then there were those who had to fight for survival every day. Corruption was everywhere, from the police to the everyday systems in place. It was disheartening.

When my time in Nigeria was up, I tried to leave, but that, too, became a battle. The airport officials kept finding reasons to prevent me from boarding my flight, demanding money to let me go. Each attempt was blocked, not because I was missing anything, but because they wanted bribes. I prayed fervently, calling on the name of Jesus. I could feel the spiritual warfare around me—darkness hovering thick in the air. But God came through. On my third attempt, after much prayer and persistence, I finally made it onto my flight. I praised God because I knew I had escaped something far greater than just corruption—I had escaped a spiritual battle.

South Africa: A Contrast of Peace and Beauty

Arriving in Cape Town felt like stepping into a different world. The moment I got off the plane, I could sense the difference. Everything was smooth—no harassment, no bribes, no overwhelming stress. I breezed through immigration without anyone bothering me, and I immediately felt peace.

As I drove through the city, I was captivated by the beauty of nature. The mountains, the ocean, the gentle breeze—it was like God Himself was saying, "Welcome, my child." I checked into a hotel in the city center, and to my delight, my room had a breathtaking view of Table Mountain. Each morning, as the sun radiated over the peaks and the clouds sat perfectly on top, I could do nothing but praise God.

One of my personal goals was to climb the mountain. When I finally stood at the top, looking down at the vastness of God's creation, I felt His presence so strongly. I took a few pictures, and to my surprise, I later noticed a rainbow over me in one of them. It was as if God was saying, "I remember my promise to you." That moment was supernatural, a divine reminder that He was with me.

While Cape Town was beautiful, I also saw the brokenness. Many were living in extreme poverty, some homeless under bridges, others battling drug addiction. I prayed for them because that was all I could offer at the time. I knew there was work to be done for the Kingdom, and I believed God would lead me back in His time.

Ghana: A Nation of Warmth and Faith

After three months in South Africa, I felt the Lord leading me to Ghana, but I wasn't sure how I would get there. Finances were tight, and I needed provision. I prayed, "Lord, if it is Your will for me to go to Ghana, open the doors. If not, I will stay here in Cape Town and wait for Your direction."

The next morning, I received a call from a friend. He said, "Simone, the Lord must really love you. He woke me up and told me to check my account. When I did, I saw money, and God told me to send it to you so you can buy your ticket." I was speechless. I smiled and whispered, "Lord, thank You for answering so quickly." It was confirmation—I was going to Ghana.

I still needed to pay for two expensive COVID-19 tests—one in Cape Town and one in Ghana. I prayed again, and the next morning, I received another unexpected financial blessing, enough to cover the first test. The following day, another friend sent me the exact amount I needed for the second test. I laughed and said, "Lord, I love Your sense of humor." God was teaching me that as long as I trusted Him, He would never fail me.

When I landed in Ghana, I immediately felt peace. The first thing I noticed was the heat—it was intense! But aside from that, the atmosphere was calm. No one harassed me, and people minded their own business. The warmth of the people made me feel welcomed.

What stood out the most about Ghana was how deeply rooted it was in Christianity. From the moment I stepped outside the airport, I saw signs, car stickers, and billboards declaring the name of Jesus. Even the taxis had scriptures on their license plates. It was impossible to ignore.

During a conversation, I met someone who was frustrated by the presence of Jesus' name everywhere. He complained, "Why do my people keep talking about this Jesus? I don't believe He is real." I realized I was speaking to an unbeliever, and instead of arguing, I shared the truth about Christ with him. By the end of our conversation, he said, "I'm now waiting for my own encounter with Jesus."

Sometimes, God places us in situations that aren't about us—they're about the assignment. My journey wasn't just about seeing different countries; it was about being used for His Kingdom. I was learning that everywhere I went, God had a purpose for me being there. This passage is powerful and deeply moving. It carries a strong message of God's love, grace, and faithfulness. Below is a refined version with better flow, grammar, and clarity while maintaining your voice and passion:

So many times, we want life to be about ourselves, but God is saying, Nope, not about you right now—it's about this very important soul. If you know anything about Jesus by now, you know that even just one soul is worth saving. His love for us is undying, selfless, and unconditional—without any turning back.

Can you imagine loving someone who doesn't even care about you? Someone who is too busy doing their own thing, not even acknowledging you? Do you have the capacity to comprehend how someone could love you when you don't love them in return? Now, imagine not only loving that person but dying for them.

It's hard to understand if you're not in tune with the Word of God. But if you're new to this kind of unconditional love, you might wonder and ponder over it, trying to figure out: Why would Jesus love me so much? But I'm here to tell you—it's real, and it's here to stay forever.

So many of us still don't realize that Jesus is the same yesterday, today, and forever—unchanging and unwavering. He is the only one who can love us so much that He would lay down His life for us. Even when we didn't know Him, we were on His mind while He was on the cross.

Someone might ask, How do I know the cross is real?

Well, let me ask you this: How do you explain waking up every morning? How do you explain falling asleep at night when some people go to bed and never wake up again? Isn't it obvious that there is a supreme being—a God who never fails? A God who answers by fire?

I am here to tell you the Good News about the man from Galilee. Sometimes we already know it, but we need to be reminded. Life comes with many trials, tribulations, ups, and downs. But here's the good news: God never leaves us nor forsakes us, no matter the circumstances. And I am living proof of that.

Salvation is here, and we must receive it with open arms.

You might ask:

- How will I keep up? God is able to keep you from falling.
- How do I break free from these chains? He is a chain-breaker—I know because He broke mine.
- But how will Jesus love me after I have sold my soul? He came for lost souls.
- How do I gain Jesus' love? It's already there, and it's free.
- What if I've killed before? No excuse—He still loves you.
- What if I joined a cult? Will He still love me? A resounding yes!

Even when we are far from Him, He never stops loving us. He said, I will make a way even in the wilderness (Isaiah 43:19). The promises of Yah stand forever and will not fall to the ground. He said, Heaven and earth shall pass away, but My word will never perish (Matthew 24:35).

If you have doubts, His Word is already here to confirm and back up everything He has promised us. And it is for everyone.

Good news!

I have tasted and seen the goodness of Jesus and what He has done for me. I was once blind, but now I see. I went from darkness to light, from dust to diamond. He gave me beauty for ashes.

The love of God is evident in our lives every day. Every morning we wake up, we experience His glory and mercy. We are blessed to be partakers of His grace.

We can make a thousand excuses not to serve the Kingdom of God, but we don't make excuses when we want what we want. And yet, He still loves us.

Long story short—no matter the situation, God can handle it.

There is nothing too hard for Him to fix, and there is no broken vessel He cannot mend. He is the Potter; we are the clay. If we allow His love to flow through us, we will stop questioning His love and start walking in it.

Who carried you this far?

Who keeps you day in and day out from accidents, pitfalls, and mishaps?

Who has shielded you from bullets, both spiritual and physical?

Jesus is our shield!

I could go on and on about all the times He saved me from death and delivered me, but I am not here to boast. I am here to testify of His goodness and share what He has done. From childhood until now, He has carried me on this journey toward the prophetic.

I believe I should be bold enough to share my story with the world because God has already gone before me. He knew this day would come. He knew I would make the best out of my pain and share it as a testimony—so that someone reading this right now would be encouraged to go on.

He knew I would suffer many things before this day, but...

He also knew that I would overcome. This passage is rich with passion, conviction, and deep spiritual insight. I've taken the liberty to refine it while maintaining your voice and intensity, making it flow better with improved clarity and structure. Here's a polished version:

God Was With Me All the Way

Some might ask, Where was God when I was going through the storm? But He was right there—He knew something good would come out of my pain. He saw beyond my suffering and knew my testimony would inspire and change someone's life forever.

God gave me the strength to endure so that I could help someone else. There is a reason for everything, and God is an on-time God. He wastes nothing. He can take the worst of situations—whether in the present or the past—and somehow create the best. He is the ultimate author of our existence.

If there had been no Job in Job's time, then who would God have used for His victory? Likewise, if there were no Simone in my time, who would God use to display His power?

Oh yes—God has bragging rights!

And when you're chosen for His purpose, for His mission, and for His glory, it is not always easy. In fact, it is never a joke. You don't get to choose—when God has chosen you, you have no choice but to surrender.

As I've said before, it's not about us—it's about God's work, His glory, and His Kingdom. Some people refuse to accept this because it's too hard for them to grasp. But the sooner you realize it's not about you, the easier it will be to walk in His purpose.

You cannot escape God—I know because I tried.

I tried running away from Him like Jonah, and just like Jonah, I was swallowed up. I tried doing things my way, but it only led me to pain. My advice? Don't try to play God—you can't. He created you. He knows every fiber of your being, every thought in your mind. Destiny is destiny, and you cannot change what God has called you to be.

If God has spoken it, so shall it be.

And if you are one of those people running from your calling—good luck, because there is an arrest date for you. You cannot hide from your Maker forever. Do yourself a favor and stop running. The moment you accept His will, everything will fall into place.

How do I know?

Because I once tried to escape, and it didn't work. I did what I wanted, until my time expired. What once brought me comfort became uncomfortable. I lost control of my direction because God had taken over. He had already begun to order my steps, and there was no turning back.

How do you know when God has taken over?

- When the sound of your voice changes—you no longer speak the way you used to; your tone carries holiness.
- When your desires change—you want to live the way you used to, but suddenly, you just can't.
- When the music you once loved no longer moves you.
- When the clothes and hairstyles you once admired no longer appeal to you.

- When you lose interest in the streets, the parties, and the people who once held your attention.
- When your heart no longer beats for a boyfriend or girlfriend—but for Jesus.
- When idle talk and gossip lose their appeal, and you crave the Word of God.
- When you suddenly find yourself thirsty for righteousness.

That, my friend, is God's intervention.

When you try to go back to your old ways but find that backsliding no longer works—that is God ordering your steps.

When you go to one last party and feel nothing—when the music no longer moves you, when you try to dance but your body won't respond the way it used to, when you embarrass yourself instead of enjoying the moment—that is God working in you.

You leave that party thinking, What just happened? I used to be the best dancer, but now I can't even keep up!

Well, news flash—it's not you. It's the God in you.

He is cleaning you up completely. You are no longer who you used to be—you are becoming a new creation in Christ Jesus.

Some have yet to experience this transformation, but your time is coming.

When Jesus Shows Up, Everything Shakes

When the disciples were on the boat, a terrible storm arose. They panicked. Then, suddenly, Jesus showed up.

At first, they thought He was a ghost. They were afraid. But it was the move of God.

When God starts moving in your life, it comes with shaking, with fear, with the unexpected. If everything remained the same, you wouldn't recognize His presence. But when things begin to spin out of control, pay attention—God might be calling you.

Sometimes, God has to shake things up in your life to get your attention.

I have realized something: When there is shaking, there is cleansing. When God wants your attention, He will shake you out of your comfort zone.

And if you've felt like your world is shaking lately, maybe it's God saying, Hello, I need you.

Crisis Can Lead to Deliverance

Have you ever noticed that when there is a crisis, there is also a recovery? That's because crisis naturally gets our attention—it forces us to run to God.

If a crisis is what it takes to bring you to Him, God will allow it.

Look at Saul, who later became Paul the Apostle. On his way to Damascus to kill God's people, he had an unexpected encounter with God. He lost his sight.

In the natural world, that would seem like a disaster. But in the spiritual world, it was divine intervention. God needed to get his attention, and He did.

Sometimes, we are so committed to darkness without even realizing it. But God loves us too much to leave us there. He will do whatever it takes to bring us into His light.

Satan's Deception

Satan, on the other hand, is always working against us while pretending to work with us. He is a liar, and there is no truth in him. He will go as far as to create something that looks like the truth—but it is not.

The Bible says, Out of the abundance of the heart, the mouth speaks.

You can tell who a person serves by the way they live. Some people lie so much that they start believing their own lies. Some lie out of habit—they can't help it.

Who is the father of lies? Satan.

Who is the way, the truth, and the life? Jesus.

There is no in-between.

The Bible says, Give unto God what is God's and unto Caesar what is Caesar's.

Joshua 24:15 says, Choose this day whom you will serve.

It is a choice.

So don't argue with me when I say, whoever your father is, that's who you will behave like.

If you belong to Jesus, you will reflect His truth. Great! I'll refine your writing for clarity, structure, and impact while keeping your voice and passion intact. Here's a revised version:

The Power of Truth and Transformation

One thing I've come to understand under the sun is this: you cannot give what you don't have. Many of us enter relationships—whether friendships, marriages, or partnerships—expecting something from a person that they simply do not have to give. This is a deep revelation.

For instance, if you're in a relationship with someone who is not saved, meaning they have not been delivered and do not have the Spirit of God within them, how can you expect them to give you godly love, truth, or righteousness? You can only receive what is in them to give. Yet, many people become frustrated when they don't receive what they desire from others, not realizing that what they seek is absent in that person. The reality is, if someone does not have the Spirit of Truth, there is no guarantee that truth will come from them. Even those who walk with God sometimes struggle to be truthful—so how much more someone who does not know Him?

This is a major issue in the world today. We set ourselves up for disappointment by expecting something that isn't there. Relationships become dead ends because we keep asking for something that doesn't exist within the other person. But how many of us are willing to admit this truth? Instead of acknowledging reality, we keep trying to make things work, even when the signs are clear. The Bible says, "Can two walk together, unless they agree?" (Amos 3:3). Light and darkness have nothing in common; they do not mix.

We must be honest with ourselves. If we truly desire the life God has promised—a life of peace, joy, prosperity, holiness, and righteousness—we must stop deceiving ourselves. We cannot expect a life of truth if we surround ourselves with lies. Yet, in today's world, many people reject truth because it challenges them. If you speak the truth, you will be questioned. If you lie, you will be accepted. Isn't that a sad reality? Some people love lies because they are familiar with deception. Just as truth recognizes truth, dishonesty recognizes dishonesty.

A thief knows another thief when he sees one. A liar can identify another liar with ease. Similarly, a person filled with the Spirit of Truth can discern truth in others. This is not rocket science—it is spiritual awareness.

A Personal Story on Lying

Some years ago, I had a friend—a guy I spent a lot of time with. Over time, I began to notice something disturbing: he was a habitual liar. He lied so much that it became a concern to me. I started wondering, If he continues this way, how will he raise his children? Will he teach them to lie too?

One day, as he was lying to me as usual, I noticed he couldn't even look me in the eyes. His body language gave him away. It was as if the truth in me was confronting the deception in him. So, I asked him to sit down and talk to me honestly. I asked him why he lied so much and where this habit came from.

To my surprise, he had an explanation. He told me that when he was younger, his grandmother treated him harshly. To avoid her wrath, he learned to lie. Every time he got caught doing something, he would lie to escape punishment. Over time, lying became second nature to him—it became his way of survival. What he didn't realize was that he had picked up a lying spirit through his pain.

This is why we must be careful. Pain can trigger all sorts of unhealthy behaviors in our lives. Many of us are carrying habits, fears, and attitudes that were birthed in our struggles. But we don't have to stay that way. The grace of God can renew our minds and transform our hearts. We must allow Him to heal us so we don't pass down dysfunction to the next generation.

Children look up to us as examples of how to live. If we have nothing good to offer them, how can we expect the next generation to be better? What we go through in life is not just for us—it's for those coming after us. That's why we need to let God transform us, so we can become vessels of truth, love, and righteousness.

Final Thoughts

We must stop playing games with ourselves. We must stop believing lies just because they feel comfortable. Truth may be hard to accept at first, but it is what sets us free. Jesus said, "I am the way, the truth, and the life" (John 14:6). If we belong to Him, then we must walk in truth, no matter how challenging it may be.

So, ask yourself today:

- Am I expecting something from people that they do not have to give?
- Am I deceiving myself about the reality of my relationships?
- Am I walking in truth, or am I just embracing what is familiar?

It's time to be honest. It's time to let God do the deep work in us. When we allow His truth to transform us, we will no longer settle for lies—we will walk boldly in His light.!

but for our children and our children children's and they are the ones that will grow to become the future of tomorrow so whatever input in them is what they will output and teach their children, it will go a long way from generation to generation and they will be tomorrow when we are no more so if we want better people be careful of you raising these little ones they are watching us and role modeling us we cannot teach them evil and expect them to do good whatever you put in that's what you will get out, that is why if you notice very well a newborn baby knows nothing until they start walking and talking you will notice a little baby if you roll over on your belly the baby will be watching you and will also attempt to do the same exact thing you're doing imitating the mother or the father so don't ever think they are not watching you, their future is in God's hand but second the parents hands so always remember that please, i have seen this myself because i did it when i was a little girl if i see my mother putting on high heels i will also push my tiny foot into her shoe that can't even fit me just following what i see my mother doing so yes it happens you can argue that is not always the case but the bottom line is they are watching you and watching what you watch i know of two girls who from a young age started practicing Lesbianism because they saw the mom and dad watching pornography on the tv and when the mom and dada is not around they began to watch it on their own and the have sense enough to hide it from the mom and dad what they were watching now they are practicing something else because of that one mistake the parents made so please parents stop this thing in front of your little ones and stop sleeping with them in the same bed while you make out and stop saying they are sleeping because that is not always the case, get them their own room if you can. there's so many little mistakes we make as parents that become big problems tomorrow and thought we might not be able to fix it all in one day or fix it all try to correct the ones you can God has given us the grace to do many things including raising our children and if you find yourself tired and slipping away ask God to help you ask for more of his grace ask him to give the wisdom the knowledge and the understanding you need for your

marriage and your children and yah will grant your request, in the book of James 4:2 it says we have not because we ask not or we ask amiss, so please ask God for these and he will grant you to raise Ladies and Gentlemen of tomorrow and men and women of God.Some trust in horses some trust in chariots i will remember the name of our Lord Psalm 20:7 in spite of what have been through i never allow it to bring me down or stop serving the Lord i continue on the journey because greater is he that is me than he that is in the world and i didn't let my pain take my integrity i didn't let it take away kindness from my spirit and i didn't let it stop me from loving i have friends that ask me before why am i so foolish i ask why and the reply was even when i get hurt by some i still show them love and i still have the ability to love again some never love again after one bad experience but i what say is this it is not me that love but the christ in me that love the christ in me knows what it is to be betrayed and treated so badly and yet still love will be flowing from his lions i told you before when you carry a certain spirit whatever the spirit is it manifest in you so i can boldly say it is not me but christ in me and to God be all the glory some of my friends and also argue that i forgive easily but when i think about what the scriptures says it makes sense forgive and you will be forgiven it's a principle a kingdom principle you don't need to hate the ones who hurt and cause you pain because it is not them that cause the pain but the spirit in them that do the damages to your heart so no need having them up as i have said before forgiveness is for yourself not just the offender show them love and the love you show them will indeed overcome the darkness let me share this testimony i was abused violated wrongfully when i was a little girl one day while alone and the guy who did it i forgot all about him and also the abuse he did i guess some part of me have already forgiven him not that it was not wrong or it didn't cause hurt and pain but i forgot about it, it was not on my mind again then one day i stumbled across the guy on the internet and he message me on facebook saying hi and how was i doing i replied calmly and without hate and he started chatting with me until he ask me for my number he said he wanted to meet up with me and i was so confident in myself i didn't feel fear or hate like i said the first thing i was thinking was how can i minister to this lost soul so i was thinking of way to spread the gospel of love to him because i believe everyone need salvation in spite of who they are and what they have done jesus said he has died for us while we were sinner and without him, for

the sinners and not the righteous so the young man ask that i accompany him somewhere where he was actually looking for an apartment in y area so i followed him and i was not mean to him or anything like that i showed him love the love of christ in me and to my surprise and my consciousness he said he want to apologize to me for something and i asked what was it and he said i remember what i did to you when you were smaller it was wrong but i don't know what came over me or pushed me to do it but i am so sorry to have done that to you and sorry for any pain i caused you and i said to the guy i forgive a long time ago and i'm sure he was relieved to hear that he must have been struggling with that sin for years because this was sixteen years later after the deed was done and God must have spoken to his conscience or it could be that he was having sleepless nights and no peace because sometimes when these people do these acts sometimes they do realize after a while that it was wrong and sometimes they can be really sorry but how will the person who you offend know your sorry if you don't find them and ask for forgiveness, and i believe it's not by my power but by the grace of God upon my life how would have known that sixteen years later this guy would come and right his wrong it is God not me because many don't get a chance to say sorry some died before they could see the person they molested to say sorry and they most likely die and go to hell for such wickedness and so many people have been hurt just like this and they never dream of the seeing the person to come and apologize to them but God must really love this young man to grant him the grace to see me to repent so i say this to share and inspire someone that might have gone through the same thing as me don't give up be encourage God is not sleeping he sees every deed that has been done and i also why i share is to demonstrate the power of love and forgiveness most people probably would have reacted so badly after seeing the person who cause you pain sixteen years earlier in your life some probably would have hire an assassin to take him out some would not have given him the chance to talk to them talk much more for coming close to them or hugging them but this is what grace does for us in our life.this is not the first time i experience something like this because if been reading this book carefully you would know this not the first time but some of those men that violated me must have died by now i don't think they are still alive truth is i don't know if they are alive but honestly i can talk about it and share it because i am healed from my scars and two i have

forgiven them i have learn to exercise the power of forgiveness because if they can do something so terrible to a child and continue live until they die what benefit do i get not forgiving them i'm just hurting myself more by just keep holding on to the pain but i'm not saying it will be this easy for everyone to forgive or even let this kind of pain go but if this happens to you and your reading please find it your heart to forgive this person who hurt and caused you pain i release in the name of Jesus as you read the grace to forgive your abusers and accusers and those who have gone through the violation of rape and molestation forgive them for your sake and also your healing process to begin i know it is not easy and i know what it feels like and that is why i can say how it feels and i have learn and gotten the grace to forgive them so i know you can in Jesus name, because carrying this weight honestly it is a very heavy burden to carry, and it is not easy some times you want to move on but it's hard, But

Let It Go and Step Into Freedom.

The pain may be staring you in the face, making it hard to let go. The enemy doesn't want you to release it because he knows that your deliverance is tied to your forgiveness. He wants you to live with shame, to hold onto bitterness, so he can keep whispering, "Look what they did to you. How can you just let it go?"

But as the Lord lives, I tell you today: let it go. Release the hurt and watch your breakthrough spring forth.

And I'm not just talking about rape or molestation—I'm talking about any pain that has been holding you captive. Whether it's heartbreak, betrayal, dishonesty, false accusations, mockery, or deep wounds from those you trusted, let it go. Let love lead the way. Open the door to healing and new beginnings.

I never thought I would be the one saying this because what I've been through is no joke—it's no child's play, no walk in the park. These are things that could have scarred me for life, things that could have left me bitter, angry, and full of hatred. But God gave me the grace to forgive. And if He can do it for me, I know He can do it for you too. You are strong in the Lord, and with Christ, all things are possible.

I have seen too many people living in bondage because of unforgiveness. They have gone through terrible pain, yet they refuse to let it go. They refuse to forgive, not realizing that their unforgiveness is keeping them in darkness. It is blocking their breakthrough. It is holding back their deliverance.

But at the end of the day, our goal should not be to please man, but to please God. We want to live the best life that He has for us. And that life requires a heart free from bitterness.

I can name almost every pain I have endured—betrayal, false accusations, rape, molestation, heartbreak, disappointment, and lies spoken against me. Yet I have overcome in the name of the Lord—not by my own might, but by the power of the Holy Spirit and by His grace.

God has given us the power to overcome, but if we lack the wisdom to do so, we must ask Him. James 1:5 tells us, "If any of you lacks wisdom, let him ask of God, who gives generously to all without reproach, and it will be given to him."

I understand more than anyone that it hurts. But if I can forgive, you can too.

One of the greatest freedoms that comes with forgiveness is peace of mind. A clear conscience. The ability to live unburdened by the weight of resentment.

I won't pretend that the journey of forgiveness is easy. When I first started, it felt awkward. Sometimes, I even found myself apologizing first, even when I wasn't the one who was wrong. But I realized something powerful: you don't have to wait for the other person to say sorry before you move on.

Start with yourself. Forgive your offender. Let God handle the rest. And watch Him move in your life. Here's the continuation of your passage with clarity, structure, and a compelling flow:

The Power of Letting Go

Forgiveness is not always easy. In fact, it can feel impossible when the pain is staring you in the face, tempting you to hold on. The enemy doesn't want you to let go because he knows that once you do, your breakthrough will come. He wants you to live with shame, to keep replaying the hurt, to never move forward.

But today, in the name of Jesus, I tell you: Let it go.

Watch how your healing begins. Watch how your life changes when you release the hurt, the betrayal, the heartbreak, the lies, the accusations, the mockery. No matter how deep the wound is—whether it's from a dishonest friend, a false accuser, or someone who violated your trust—let it go and let love lead.

I never thought I'd reach a day where I could speak about my pain with peace in my heart. What I have been through is no joke—it's not child's play. These are wounds that could have scarred me for life, filled me with hatred and bitterness. But by God's grace, I overcame. Not by my strength, but by His power.

I have seen so many people trapped in bondage because of unforgiveness. They've been through terrible things, yet they refuse to release the pain. They don't even realize that their unforgiveness is holding them back from their blessings, their healing, and their destiny.

Unforgiveness is a heavy weight. It delays breakthroughs. It hinders deliverance. It keeps you from living the life God has for you.

But when you forgive, you step into freedom.

I could list every betrayal, every false accusation, every violation, every disappointment. But I won't—because I am no longer defined by them. I have overcome them through Christ, not by my might, but by the power of the Holy Spirit and the grace of God.

Forgiveness Brings Freedom

Some might argue, "But it hurts too much to forgive."

Oh, I know that pain very well. But if I can do it, so can you.

One of the greatest blessings of forgiveness is peace of mind. A clear conscience. True freedom.

At first, when I started my journey of forgiveness, it felt awkward. Sometimes, I even found myself saying sorry first—even when I wasn't wrong. But I realized something: Forgiveness is not about who is right or wrong; it is about being free.

There are people in this world who will never admit their faults. They will never apologize. Their pride won't allow them to. But if you wait for them to say sorry before you move forward, you are giving them power over your life.

Don't wait. Forgive them anyway.

Release it, and watch God take care of the rest. Here's a refined version of your passage with improved clarity, structure, and grammar while keeping your voice and message intact:

I used to hold on to the pain, constantly replaying the things my adopted mother did to me. She treated me like I was nothing, even giving me dog food as if I were an animal. The bitterness and unforgiveness weighed me down. But thank God, I found the strength to forgive her. And after I did, something unexpected happened—she became sick, and she never recovered.

I was far away, living my own life, when one day, while working out and listening to music, I heard the Holy Spirit whisper to me, "Your mother is going to pass away." The words shocked me. I stopped what I was doing, and sadness washed over me. I began to cry, mourning her before she was even gone.

That moment showed me something—I had truly forgiven her. Despite everything she had done to me, I loved her. I cared for her, pampered her, even when she treated me like I was nothing. I couldn't understand it at the time, but now I know: the love inside me was greater than the hate she showed me.

I used to wonder why she resented me so much when all I ever did was love her. But when the Lord revealed to me that she was leaving this earth, I wasn't happy. Some people might have felt relieved, considering how she had treated them, but I wasn't. Instead, I cried for her. That was when I knew—I had conquered unforgiveness.

There was a time when I struggled with it. I constantly checked my heart, asking myself, "Did I really forgive her? How do I know for sure?" I didn't want her to die while I was still holding on to bitterness. I even prayed for a sign. And when that moment of grief came, when I mourned for her despite everything, I knew I had let go.

She passed away without ever asking for my forgiveness. But I had already given it. And that's why I say—don't wait for an apology. Some people will never say sorry. Some will die with pride, never admitting their wrongs. But that shouldn't stop you from forgiving. Do it for yourself.

I don't know what was in her heart before she died. Maybe she wanted to apologize but never got the chance. Sometimes, people suffer in their final days because God is giving them time to make things right. He doesn't want anyone to perish, so He gives us opportunities to repent.

Through all the pain, the shame, the betrayals, the false accusations, the heartbreaks, the violations, the near-death experiences—God brought me through. I didn't think I would make it, but I did. Not by my own strength, but by His power.

I saw my death so many times, yet God didn't allow it. I should have died when the doctor told me, "If you had waited until tomorrow, you wouldn't have survived." But God said, "Not yet."

I was on the edge of a rooftop, ready to give up on life, but God was there.

I was in a car that spun out of control, heading straight for a bus, but God was there.

I had two motor accidents in one week, yet I walked away unharmed. That was God.

So many times, I almost got hit by a car, yet something always stopped it from happening. That was God.

Even when I couldn't see Him, He was always near.

I take no credit for surviving. I give all the glory to God because He is the one who kept me. His grace covered me, His strength upheld me, and His love carried me through. And now, for the rest of my days, I will do the work of the Lord until He calls me home.

This is my assignment. Here's a refined version of your passage with improved structure, clarity, and grammar while keeping your heartfelt message intact:

Everything I share in this book is not to put anyone down but to educate, encourage, and inspire God's people—the ones He so desperately wants to reach. This book is for edification, and I take no glory for myself because God's strength is proven in our weakness.

For a long time, I didn't fully understand what that meant until I found myself in situations where I desperately needed His strength. Sometimes, God allows us to go through trials so that His power can be revealed in our weakest moments. I'm not saying I know everything or have experienced everything, but I have been through a lot. And by the grace of God, I've survived.

The things I've endured should have broken me, but instead, they have become a testimony. I don't look like what I've been through, and that's the power of God's grace. Grace gives you the ability to walk through storms without looking like the storm itself.

I want you to take this story and let it inspire and encourage you. Even if it doesn't seem relevant today, there may come a time when you need this testimony. Writing this book wasn't easy—it was a battle, spiritually, physically, and emotionally. That's how I know it will help someone. Maybe not today, maybe not tomorrow, but one day.

This book is special because it took me eleven years to write it. Four times, I lost the materials, and on the fifth attempt, I succeeded—by the grace of God. Nothing happens before its time, and now is the time for this story to be released. God wanted me to be in the right frame of mind, with the right spirit, before I could write it. And now, here it is—ready for you.

I didn't endure all of this just for myself. I didn't fight to write this book for no reason. This is for you, for me, and for the glory of God. So take your time, sip your favorite tea, and read on. If you've made it this far, know that there's something in this book for you—or maybe for someone you know. If you don't feel like this message is for you, share it with a friend or a family member. Someone needs to hear this.

And if you take nothing else from this book, please remember this: Jesus loves you. Tell someone else this message—someone who needs to hear it today.

Another reason I took my time writing this book is because of your soul. It matters where you and I go after this life. I don't want to see you lose your soul. Hell is real, and I don't want you to end up there. Please, seek Jesus while you still have the chance. If you once walked with Him but drifted away, come back—before it's too late.

Salvation is free. The love of Jesus is free. And it is your key to everlasting life and peace.

If you're tired of the enemy's lies...

If you're tired of torment, sadness, depression, and bondage...

There is a way out.

And that way is Jesus Christ.

He is the way, the truth, and the life.

If you want the peace, freedom, and divine protection I've talked about—if you're ready to be on the winning side—then say this prayer with me:

Lord Jesus, You died on the cross and rose again on the third day. Because You live, I can live. Thank You for Your sacrifice. Lord, I am a sinner. Please forgive me, come into my heart, and be my Savior. In Jesus' name, Amen.

If you just prayed this prayer, congratulations! You are now part of the family of Christ. Heaven is rejoicing, and so am I! Welcome to the winning side!

Let the love of God reign in your heart today and forever.

Thank you all for your love and support, and to God be the glory for making this book possible.

I love you all. Shalom.

God has given me the strength to overcome darkness. His grace has kept me time and time again. I have seen my own death so many times, yet God did not allow me to die—because it was not my time. There is work for me to do here on Earth.

And if you join me—if we work together—so much can be accomplished for the Kingdom of Heaven.

For the rest of my living days, I want to do Yah's work until He returns. That is my assignment.

Everything I share in this book is not to condemn anyone but to educate, encourage, and inspire God's people. He longs to reach you. This book is for edification, and I take no glory for myself—because God's strength is proven in our weakness.

Honestly, I never fully understood what that meant until I was in a situation where I needed His strength. Sometimes, God allows us to go through trials so that His strength can be revealed in our weakest moments.

I'm not saying I know everything or that I have experienced everything. But I have been through a lot. And like many others, I have faced hardships—but with Christ by my side, I made it through. By His strength and grace, I endured.

And yet, I don't look like what I've been through.

That's what grace does for you.

It gives you the ability to weather storm after storm, yet you don't look like your storms.

I want you to take this story and let it inspire and encourage you. I know it will help you someday—maybe not today, but when you need it most.

Do you know why?

Because writing this testimony was not easy.

Spiritually, physically, and emotionally, it was a battle. That's how I know it will help someone—it was fought for.

Let me tell you why this book is so special:

It took me eleven years to get this testimony into writing—for you. That special someone who needs this message.

Four times, I lost the materials for this book. But on the fifth attempt, I succeeded—by the grace of God.

Nothing happens before its time.

And the time is now.

God wanted me to be in the right frame of mind and the right spirit to write this book. And now is that time.

I did not endure all these trials just for myself. I did not fight to write this book for no reason.

This book is for you, for me, and for God's victorious glory.

So please, take your time. Sip your favorite tea. Read on.

And if you've read this far, it's for you.

There is something in this testimony for you or for someone you know.

If it doesn't seem meant for you, share it with a friend—it may be exactly what they need.

God loves you.

That is the message I want you to know.

And please, tell someone else: Jesus loves them.

Another reason I took the time to write this book is because of your soul.

It is very important where you and I go after this life.

I do not want to see you lose your soul and end up in hell.

Hell is real.

So please, seek Jesus Christ while you still can—before it's too late.

If you have never repented, or if you once walked with God but have since strayed, let me remind you:

Salvation is free.

This love is free.

And it is your key to everlasting life and peace.

If you are tired—tired of the enemy's lies, tired of the torment, tired of sadness, depression, and bondage—there is a way out.

And that way is Jesus.

Jesus is the way, the truth, and the life.

If you want peace, freedom, and constant covering—if you want someone to fight your battles for you so you no longer have to keep losing—then choose Jesus.

And if you are ready, say this simple prayer with me:

> Lord Jesus,
>
> You died on the cross, and You rose again on the third day.
>
> Because You live, I live.
>
> Thank You for the sacrifice You made for me.
>
> Lord Jesus, I am a sinner.
>
> Please forgive me of my sins and come into my heart and my life—today and forever.
>
> In Jesus' name, Amen.
>
> If you just prayed that prayer—congratulations!
>
> You are now part of the family of Christ. You are on the winning side.
>
> Welcome, welcome, welcome!
>
> Let the love of Almighty God reign in your heart today and forever.
>
> Thank you, everyone, for your love and support. And to God be the glory for making this book possible.
>
> Love to all.
>
> Shalom.

God was right there with me when I was sick and near death. The doctor told me that if I had waited until the next day, I would have died—but God saved my life right then and there.

He was with me when I stood on the edge of a rooftop, ready to give up because my life felt so depressing. He was there when my car spiraled out of control and nearly crashed into a bus—but it didn't, because God said, Not yet.

When I had two car accidents in one week and walked away unharmed—that was God. When I almost got hit by a car multiple times, yet each time, I was spared—that was God.

You see, God is always there, just as He promised. Sometimes, we can't see Him, so we believe He is distant. But far be it from the truth! The way you know God is with you is when you go through these moments and look back, realizing you couldn't have made it alone. He is our shade at our right hand.

But when you're walking through the valley, it doesn't always feel like God is there. Still, He is ever near.

I take no credit or glory for myself—to God be all the glory for keeping me and giving me the strength to overcome darkness. By His grace, I have seen death many times, yet He did not allow me to die because my time had not yet come. There is work for me to do here on Earth.

And if you join me—if we work together—so much can be accomplished for the Kingdom of Heaven.

For the rest of my living days, I want to do Yah's work until He returns. That is my assignment.

Everything I share in this book is not to put anyone down but to educate, encourage, and inspire God's people. It is for edification, and I take no glory because God's strength is proven in our weakness.

Honestly, I never fully understood what that meant until I was in a situation where I needed His strength. Sometimes, God allows us to go through trials so that His strength can be made perfect in our weakest moments.

I am not saying I know everything or have been through everything, but I have been through a lot. And by Christ's strength and grace, I have endured what many others face—and yet, I don't look like what I've been through. That's what grace does for you—it gives you the ability to go through storm after storm, yet you don't look like your storms.

I want you to take this story and let it inspire and encourage you. I know it will help you someday when you need it the most. Do you know why? Because writing this testimony was not easy. Spiritually, physically, and emotionally, it was a battle. That's how I know it will help someone—it was fought for.

Maybe not today, but one day, these words will speak to you. And let me tell you why this book is so special:

It took me eleven years to get this testimony into writing—for you. That special someone who needs this message.

Four times, I lost the materials for this book. But on the fifth attempt, I succeeded—by the grace of God.

Nothing happens before its time. And the time is now.

God wanted me to be in the right frame of mind and the right spirit to write this book. And now is that time.

I did not endure all these trials just for myself. I did not fight to write this book for no reason. It is for you and me—and for God's victorious glory.

So please, take your time. Sip your favorite tea. Read on.

And if you've read this far, it's for you. There is something in this testimony for you or for someone you know. So if it doesn't seem meant for you, share it with a friend—it may be exactly what they need.

God loves you.

That is the message I want you to know.

And please, tell someone else: Jesus loves them.

Another reason I took the time to write this book is because of your soul.

It is very important where you and I go after this life.

I do not want to see you lose your soul and end up in hell. Hell is real. So please, seek Jesus Christ while you still can—before it's too late.

If you have never repented, or if you once walked with God but have since strayed, let me remind you: Salvation is free. This love is free. And it is your key to everlasting life and peace.

If you are tired—tired of the enemy's lies, tired of the torment, tired of sadness, depression, and bondage—there is a way out.

And the way is Jesus.

Jesus is the way, the truth, and the life.

If you want that peace, that freedom, that constant covering—if you want someone to fight your battles for you so that you no longer have to keep losing—then choose Jesus.

And if you are ready, say this simple prayer with me:

> Lord Jesus,
>
> You died on the cross, and You rose again on the third day.

Because You live, I live.

Thank You for the sacrifice You made for me.

Lord Jesus, I am a sinner.

Please forgive me of my sins and come into my heart and my life—today and forever.

In Jesus' name, Amen.

If you just prayed that prayer—congratulations!

You are now part of the family of Christ. You are on the winning side.

Welcome, welcome, welcome!

Let the love of Almighty God reign in your heart today and forever.

Thank you, everyone, for your love and support. And to God be the glory for making this book possible.

Love to all. Shalom.

Printed in the United States
by Baker & Taylor Publisher Services